# The Adventures of Bella & Emily

# The Adventures of Bella & Emily

* * *

*Michelle Lesley Holland*

Cover design by Sam Wall

This book is dedicated to my Mum, Sonya Holland and to my dear friend Ena Webster. My
Mum always inspired me to follow my dreams and Ena supported and encouraged me to write
this book. I am very sad that neither are no longer with us. They are both a big part of this book
so their memories will live on. Thank you also to Lee Marsh and Sue Morris for all of your help
and input over the last four years.
ISBN-13: 9781544653310
ISBN-10: 154465331X

# Chapter 1

* * *

I AM CANTERING BAREBACK THROUGH the dense woods; the sun is glistening through the branches of the trees. I gently squeeze my pony; she immediately responds and we gallop towards a beautiful green field. I look up into the deep blue sky and see beautiful pony shape clouds floating around. It feels like Heaven.

My alarm is beeping loudly in my ears, a bright light is shining directly at me. I groan loudly and fling one arm across my eyes to shield the early morning sun, using my other one to try and turn off the ear-splitting noise. Why did I forget to draw my bedroom curtains last night?

"Bother," I groan once again as I grab a handful of bed covers to pull over my head.

It's no use, I'm fully awake. There is absolutely no chance of me being able to drift back into my dream so I might as well get up. I am feeling very annoyed as I was thoroughly enjoying my dream.

My name is Emily Pope, and as far back as I can remember, my one and only dream has been to own my own pony. Not just any old pony mind you. I know exactly what I want. My pony will be a golden dun in colour, have beautiful dark markings on her legs, and a long dark flowing mane. After months and months of agonizing, trying to think of the perfect name, one day completely out of the blue, it came to me, Bella. My pony will be called Bella.

I fling back the bed covers and spring out of bed. I really do hope I will be able to resume my dream tonight.

"Bella, Bella, Bella, my beautiful Bella," I sing aloud, as I get washed and dressed.

I am now ready to start my day.

I am thirteen years old, five foot two inches tall and I live with my parents in a lovely bungalow in Friston, a quaint little village in East Sussex.

My bedroom is situated at the rear, and looks out onto the stunning South Downs. Home to me means a magnificent view, a garden full of cherry blossom in the spring, and plenty of peace and quiet. You might think this is a bit weird for a thirteen year old girl, but that's just the way I like it.

I have a passion for nature and adore almost every living creature although I will confess, I actually detest spiders. I hate their pitch black hairy legs, and prefer it if they keep themselves to themselves.

One thing I do have a passion for though, is ants. The reason? Well, I have two Nans, and from as far back as I can remember Nan H would regularly say to me, "Emily dear, sit still child. You're doing the ants-in-your-pants, belly-button dance again." I've never been able to understand how ants can make my belly-button dance. Still, if Nan H said they do, then I believe her, but to this very day I still find it puzzling.

Down a slope at the bottom of the garden is a small wooded area. It's overgrown and is full of extraordinary things, most of which haven't been touched in years. There's part of a statue, an old welly boot, a very old tin kettle a robin has used to make her nest in, and a large ant colony residing by the big oak tree nearby.

A short distance away, monkey puzzle trees, pine trees and huge sycamore trees teem with life. The sycamore trunks have the most amazing knotty patterns on their bark. They soar high into the sky, just shy of Heaven. A run down shed sits all alone-except for wall to wall spiders and their silky webs. Mice and other creatures creep around inside and make it their home. No-one has been brave enough to venture inside this shed for ages; not me, not my friends, nor any grown-up, as far as I know.

I have my own secret hideaway tucked out of sight just behind these grand trees. My special place holds secrets only the trees know because I talk to them. I love watching the leaves change colour through the seasons. The vibrant green leaves change to golden brown, then effortlessly fall to the ground. I love the scrunching noise they make as I walk over them. I spend endless summer days in my hideaway dreaming about my Bella, smiling as I watch the colourful wild flowers dance in the soft gentle breeze.

"Emily, Sophie's here," Mum calls to me from the kitchen.

"Okay mum, I'm just coming," I shout as I make my way to the kitchen wondering if I should show Sophie my secret hideaway. But would she keep my secret?

"Hello Sophie," I say cheerfully. "Shall we go out into the garden? It's much too nice a day to stay indoors."

"Fine by me," agrees Sophie.

Mrs Pope stands at the window and watches the two girls make their way down the garden path. *'I wonder what mischief those two will get up to today'*, she thinks to herself.

I stop at the end of the path and turn to face Sophie and ask her in a serious voice, "Sophie, can you keep a secret?"

"If I have to, then yes I can," she confirms. "I just love secrets."

Nodding my head I take the lead, "Follow me, I want to show you somewhere very special to me."

We walk down the steep path through the small gate at the bottom, and into the large wooded area. I stand still with my legs spread apart, throw my arms open wide in a grand gesture and look at Sophie, "Well what do you think?" I really hope Sophie loves it as much as I do.

Sophie stands still and stares, slowly she moves her head around. Her mouth is wide open. "Wow," she gasps. "I wish I had a place like this, Emily you should have shared this with me a very long time ago".

"It is pretty special, isn't it?" A big grin is spreading across my face. "When I want time to myself, this is my sanctuary. Except for that old shed over there. Not even my parents will go in there."

"Why? What's wrong with it?" Sophie asks puzzled. "It just looks old to me. Maybe if we venture inside and have a look around. You never know, we might find some long forgotten treasure."

Sophie slowly makes her way towards the shed.

"No!" I shout as I lunge forward grabbing Sophie by her arm to pull her back.

"What on earth's the matter?" laughs Sophie.

"Well, it's full of spiders, and I've noticed some huge ones coming and going from there. To be honest, I think the spiders webs are the only things keeping the old shed from collapsing altogether. Those webs can be quite strong you know."

"Are you really scared of a few spiders?" Sophie asks, grinning at me.

I have no intention of admitting to her how much spiders terrify me, and try to put a brave face on this situation.

"Alright then, we'll have a quick look," I agree. "But you go first. I'll be right behind you."

Sophie takes a deep breath and continues to walk towards the shed. The door is slightly ajar, and she gingerly tries to pull it open. It's well and truly stuck. Tugging at the door with both hands, she manages to open it a few inches. She repositions herself to the other side of the door, takes a deep breath, braces herself and gives it a good pull. The door groans, creaks and bends alarmingly. I'm a bit worried it's going to fall to bits but before long it slowly scrapes across the mud and leaves which have gathered around the base.

Finally, the door is fully open, and we both peer inside. Cob webs are hanging everywhere, and a very large dusty one runs from one beam to another making it look like a hammock. I can't help but giggle as my imagination takes over. I have a picture in my head, a family of mice are enjoying themselves as they lay on their backs gently swinging in the hammock with their little legs high in the air.

Sophie tentatively puts one foot inside. I can see she isn't as brave as she makes out to be, and I can't stop myself lightly running my fingers through her hair. She almost jumps out of her skin, screams loudly, and as she turns to run, knocks me over in her haste to get away. I don't waste any time either in scrabbling to my feet, and I run after her.

"You gave me such a fright," screeches Sophie slapping me on my arm once we come to a halt and we both sink down onto the grass to lay in the beautiful sunshine. We burst out laughing, in fact a touch of hysterics to be honest, probably releasing our nervous tension, and it takes a while before we calm down.

"Come on Sophie, I'll show you more of my secret hideaway."

We jump to our feet and I lead the way down a nearby slope, the sun is shining brightly. Phew not a spider in sight.

Suddenly Sophie shrieks and is now running away up the slope.

"What's the matter? Where are you going? Sophie come back, what's wrong?" I shout.

"S-Snake!" she yells over her shoulder but carries on running.

"What?"

Once she is at the top of the slope, she turns to look at me, her hands are on her hips and she is bent over trying to get her breath back. Standing up straight, she points a finger to where she had been standing before, and splutters a load of nonsense.

Eventually she takes a deep breath and manages to blurt out, "There's a s-snake down there, just in front of you. I d-don't like snakes."

I look to where Sophie is pointing and head off in that direction until I reach the spot where Sophie thinks she has seen a snake. I crouch down to search in the long grass and sure enough something moves.

"Sophie, it's ok," I shout back to her. "There aren't any snakes down here, it's only a slow-worm. Look!" I carefully pick it up and hold it high enough for her to see.

"Argh," shrieks Sophie. "It's still a snake Emily," and not waiting to see any more she turns and runs in the direction of the bungalow.

Giggling to myself, I shrug my shoulders, bend down and gently place the slow worm back in the grass where it wriggles away to find a safer place to sunbathe.

I trot along after Sophie. Although I am sorry she was frightened, I now feel so much better about being scared of spiders. Everyone has a phobia I suppose.

I can see in the distance Sophie is wandering off towards the old run down barn, it sits at the bottom of the grassland not too far from the bungalow. I catch up with her and ask, "Would you like to go inside and have a look around?" "Ok" she replies "But please don't make me jump again".

Again, large dusty cobwebs circle the cold dark beams. The barn is full of storage boxes and other odds and ends. I can see it from my bedroom window, and often have visions of my Bella being housed there.

"Not today, thank you," replies Sophie, eying the barn. "I think I have had enough frights for one day, I'd better head back home."

"Alright. I'll see you in a day or two then," I reply, as I watch her make her way to the gate, waving as she goes.

# Chapter 2

FOR YEARS MY PARENTS HAVE been very aware of how I feel. They know I will never give up on my dream of one day owning my own pony.

This morning as we all sit at the old wooden bench table in the kitchen for breakfast, I think they are more than a little surprised to hear me ask them this very question.

"Mum, Dad, you both know I really, really want my own pony," I begin looking at Mum first and then Dad. My mouth has gone very dry, but I must carry on before all my courage fails me. Do you think it's possible for me to have one for Christmas?" I babble and reaching out a shaking hand I grab my glass of strawberry milkshake and take a big gulp. How I manage not to choke is beyond me.

Across the table, Dad suddenly looks up from spreading honey onto his buttered toast. He glances across to Mum and clears his throat. Not a good sign. It means he's going to be very serious and will try and break bad news gently.

"Emily you are only thirteen years old. Mum and I feel you are much too young."

I feel my face drop, and my stomach sinks.

"But…"

"Now hear me out Emily love. Owning a pony is a very serious commitment. You can't look after it one day and not the next if you don't feel like it. It will have to be looked after three hundred and sixty-five days a year, mucked out, fed, and watered. This means Christmas Day as well as holidays. You know your mother and I are much too busy with our jobs to have to fit that in as well.

"Yes Dad."

Looking closely at my face and glancing at Mum, Dad continues, "But we are willing to compromise. You will need to prove to us you are capable of caring for a pony, and in all weathers. If you can do this, well, then your dream of owning your own pony, may one day come true."

I feel hope bubbling up, and a smile is emerging across my face.

"Let me mull it over for a few days Emily, and I will speak to you again about this."

My parents have always worked very hard especially since leaving school. I am fully aware of how hard I need to work if I want my dream to come true. I want this so badly it sometimes hurts.

I can hear Dad making phone calls this afternoon. He must be really busy as he doesn't normally use the phone at home for work. Maybe he's forgotten about my pony.

It's been a few days since I had approached the subject of owning my own pony, and Mum and Dad have just called me into the kitchen. They are sitting at the kitchen table when I poke my head around the door. "Yes Mum, Dad, did you want me for something?"

"Sit down Emily love, your father has something to say."

"Sounds serious," I try to joke.

Dad drags out the nearest chair and pats it for me to sit on. "Emily, how would you like to help out at the local riding school at the weekends?"

"Are you serious? I would love to," I gush.

"That's good," says Dad smiling at me. "I've been making arrangements over the telephone with Mrs Evans, who as you know owns and runs the riding school, and she has agreed that you may start working there from this coming Saturday. You will start at the bottom and work your way up and learn as much as you can."

"Are you serious?"

"Very serious Emily love. It will be good experience for you, and show you exactly what is involved," confirms Dad.

Jumping up from the table, I more or less throw myself at Dad and give him the biggest hug I can, and a big hug for Mum too. "Thank you, thank you. I will do my very best and work hard, I promise."

"We know you will love. Now run along and get rid of some of that energy of yours before you explode with joy," laughs Dad.

Running out of the bungalow I want to jump in the air as high as I can and shout out aloud at the top of my voice. I somehow manage to contain my joy until I am safely on my way to my secret hideout. "Wow, wow, wow" I scream as I run down the hill, my arms gliding through the air. "I will be able to stroke them, touch them, smell them, I just can't wait, isn't this just GREAT," I shout to the trees and any creatures who are listening.

I have ridden my bike passed the riding school many times in the past so I know exactly where it is. I often stop outside to listen to the sounds of the horses and ponies whinnying. The smell of them makes my heart jump. Ponies are in my head constantly, day and night and, always in my dreams.

During the last year or two I've come to know some of the ponies living in the village. There are two young ponies in particular I have a very soft spot for. I've named them Bill and Ben, and they live near to the local primary school.

They are so comical to watch, always playing and having such fun together. I've wasted hours in the past watching and laughing at their behaviour. One day, the two of them were walking around and round in a circle grabbing each other's tails in their mouths. To me it looked as if they were playing 'Ring a ring o' Roses'! *Is this possible? Do they seriously know nursery rhymes?* Maybe not, but like the ants I'm not convinced.

Another day, they were playing a karate game galloping around the field together. Bill would run up to Ben's side, lean across and quickly bite poor Ben's knee-cap. This would make Ben stumble and almost fall down although he somehow managed to keep cantering, and they start playing the game all over again! *Is this part of the same nursery rhyme 'Atishoo! Atishoo! We all fall down?'* If so, how clever!

I have laughed so much; tears have rolled down my cheeks. Sometimes they wear head collars and they pull and tug each other around by the throat strap! How clever is that? A true joy to see such happy ponies.

One cold snowy day in winter, I had stopped to talk to them. Something didn't look quite right so I decided to have a closer inspection. They both had frozen icicles on their whiskers but they seemed oblivious to these as they continued munching on their hay. I laughed as they didn't seem at all concerned about their frozen beards. I'm pretty sure if I had icicles in my hair or hanging from my nose, I'd be bothered!

Due to the thickness of the snow, the weight had forced an old crumbling bird table nearby to sit at an awkward angle. This was too inviting for the comical pair. I watched as the mischievous pair leaned over as far as they could. Bill, could just about reach a fat ball hanging there and as he touched it, he curled up his top lip. I am sure he was laughing. What a great day to have had my camera with me, 'Click' superb photo. I can always guarantee these two can put a smile on my face.

Today I rush home from school in record time. Mum is driving me to the local saddlery so I can buy some jodhpurs, a riding hat, and long riding boots. My birthday was back in August and I had asked my family members if they would mind giving me money instead of presents. Thankfully they had all agreed, and today I can have a great time spending it.

It's a dismal Friday afternoon in October. I do like Friday's as it is the last day of the school week. Mum and I arrive back home from the saddlery and now I need to get my homework out of the way as quickly as possible so I can start to get ready for my very first day at the riding school.

Every week over the last two years I have helped with the household chores to earn my pocket money. My least favourite jobs are washing up and vacuuming but I never moan as it enables me to buy the items I need on my 'wish list' and these are stacking up very nicely in my bedroom cupboard.

I check through my items again, I have a complete grooming kit, a head collar, and a riding whip. "Wow, not bad," I say to nobody in particular. The money I have left over after my trips to the saddlery, sits in my water bucket, which is hidden safely at the bottom of my wardrobe. I can't help smiling. My money is nicely adding up. I have set myself a target, I need to save £900 for my *dream pony*.

Pony posters and my own drawings cover my bedroom walls. I love art, writing poetry, and lying on my bed doodling which isn't as often as I would like. I always seem to be busy doing one thing or another.

A brilliant idea has just popped into my head. I'm going to surprise Mum and Dad with a mini fashion parade wearing my new riding school outfit I bought earlier. I giggle as I pull on my jodhpurs, boots, polo neck jumper and add the final touch with my riding hat. I gallop down the hallway heading towards the lounge, I love the noise my whip makes smacking against my boots. My lips make a clicking sound as I go.

Whoopee, this is fun.

I'm really not sure how it happens, (maybe it's due to the fact that I'm not used to wearing long riding boots, and I know for sure there was nothing left lying in the hallway) but suddenly I'm tumbling forwards, I desperately try to grab hold of something, anything at all to stop me from falling and landing flat on my face but I still seem to be gathering momentum and crash through the lounge door, landing in a sprawled heap on the floor right in front of Mum and Dad.

To say they look astonished is an understatement. They sit for quite a few seconds before Dad suddenly bursts out laughing. Mum looks across at him, she cannot contain herself either and joins in too. Both of them just lose it. Mum has tears running down her face. Dad is laughing so much he is now having a coughing fit. It certainly wasn't what they were expecting to see as they were quietly watching television. I am mortified, but seeing them laugh so much, I can't help but join in. The giggles are so contagious and get out of hand. Eventually, I drag myself up and hobble back to my bedroom to get changed. I can still hear Mum and Dad laughing away in the distance.

I've been told on more than one occasion that my grin is adorable and it makes me look very cheeky. I totally agree as I look at myself up and down in the mirror.

Tomorrow I'll be spending nearly all day with ponies. The thought of this is making my tummy jump. I just know I'm going to have trouble sleeping tonight, I'm just so excited.

Putting everything neatly away, I climb into my favourite printed pony PJ's, jump into bed and instead of counting sheep I count dun coloured ponies jumping over cross-country fences. 78, 79, 80.

# Chapter 3

### * * *

ARGH! THE ALARM IS BEEPING like crazy making me jump even though I'm wide awake just lying in bed day dreaming. Stretching out an arm, I quickly turn it off. It's much too early for such an ear splitting noise.

6.30am in the morning, and I have a busy day ahead.

My first job is to do my usual paper round at 7.00am. I love it. Why? Well, for one thing it means more money to add to my pony bucket!

I spring out of bed and run across the room, pull open my curtains, and stand quietly for a couple of seconds staring out of the window. The weather is miserable. The nearby South Downs are covered in mist, but even this cannot put a dampener on today for me. I'm just too excited. I'm not due at the riding school until 9.00am so I have plenty of time.

Normally I'm as quiet as a mouse delivering the morning papers, not wanting to disturb people, but today I can't help but sing loudly as I push the papers through the letter boxes. By the time I arrive home at seven forty five, the mist is clearing and for an October morning it's very mild and my spirits are soaring.

I gallop into the kitchen to see my breakfast is sitting waiting for me on the kitchen table. I grind to a halt. Oh no, now what am

I supposed to do? I'm too excited to eat anything, I am not hungry. I nibble on a slice of toast and naughtily as Mum disappears down the hallway, I put the remainder of my breakfast into the bin. I know my Mum all too well, she would continue to moan at me. I can just hear her saying, *'You cannot go out on an empty stomach young lady,'* and she would go on and on and on. I mimic this in my head, moving my lips as I say the words, only just managing to stifle my giggles. Grinning, I shout out up the hallway "Lovely breakfast, thanks Mum!"

My riding school clothes are warming on my bedroom radiator. Mum does this with most of my clothes in the cold damp months, especially with my school uniform. It's such a lovely feeling to feel warm and cosy as I get dressed. I grab them off the radiator and get changed.

I look in the mirror to check my appearance. *"Wow,"* I say out aloud but not meaning to. *"How smart do I look?"* I hardly recognise myself. My smile turns into a huge grin as I pose at every angle possible, sideways, backwards, in fact nearly turning myself inside out. I suddenly have a feeling I am being watched and quickly turn around to see Mum chuckling away at my antics. She manages to blurt out in between her giggles, "You look very smart love."

It's now time for me to be on my way and Dad has joined Mum to say goodbye, each giving me a kiss.

"Enjoy yourself Emily and good luck. We'll look forward to hearing all about your day when you come home tonight. Please be careful," says Dad, with a big grin on his face.

I'm just about to leave through the front door when I hear Mum's voice. "Emily love, hang on, you nearly forgot your lunch box. I've made your favourite sandwiches."

"Thanks Mum, I don't know what I'd do without you," I reply as I trot back to get them from her.

*"Oh no,"* I groan to myself, this is going to be very embarrassing on my first day. My favourite sandwiches are cucumber, salad cream, covered with lots of black pepper on the top. I wonder what the others are going to say at lunchtime when I pull out my sandwiches. "Oh well," I grumble to myself, I'll have to deal with this later.

Jumping onto my bike I peddle like mad and arrive promptly at the stables at 8.30am. I want to be early; I hate being late for anything.

Padlocking my bike to the railings outside the yard I eagerly walk through the main gates, taking deep steadying breaths as I enter, holding my body upright with as much confidence as I can manage. I am walking up the pathway to the yard, my heart is beating very hard and I anxiously turn around to double check that I've shut the gate properly.

Above the gate is a big sign saying 'Reception' in fancy black letters with an arrow pointing to a building off to the right. I head in that direction and now I am standing at the main reception ringing the doorbell. I take another deep breath. 'DING DONG', no answer. I have my finger poised ready to try again when a tall thin lady with mousy brown hair suddenly opens the door.

"Hello, can I help you?" she asks in a very friendly voice.

"Good morning, my name is Emily. I'm here to see Mrs Evans."

"Come in a second. My name's Jodie and I am the head groom here. Please take a seat," she says pointing to a chair in front of the desk. "Mrs Evans will be with you shortly." I look Jodie up and down, I think she is around 30 years old and seems a very nice lady.

I sit patiently and take the opportunity to look around the office. My jaw is ajar as I glance around. Rosettes completely cover one wall, I've never seen so many. Moving my head slowly to look at the next wall, photographs of horses and ponies jumping various courses, taking part in gymkhanas, show jumping, and cross country. Some of the photographs are in colour, others are in black and white. I am now drawn to the far corner of the office to a large oak, glass-fronted cabinet. It's full of silver and gold trophies together with crystal bowls which are gleaming and sparkling in the light. I am drifting off into a day dream. I can see a big silver trophy sitting on my bedroom cabinet and rosettes completely covering my bedroom walls.

Suddenly, a voice startles me and I jump back to reality instantly.

"Hello dear, I'm Mrs Evans, what a pleasure it is to meet you."

I look up and see a very slim middle aged lady. She's wearing cream coloured jodhpurs and a very nice expensive looking riding jacket.

I can't help noticing she's wearing far too much make up. In fact, it's a big possibility she must have been in a real hurry this morning as her bright red lipstick is lop sided, and even worse, she has quite a bit of it smudged on her chin! I'm trying so hard not to laugh and decide to focus on something else, the best thing for me to do at this present moment, is to look away quickly.

Mrs Evans holds out a thin right hand which I eagerly grasp and shake. She has a very strong handshake herself, and I think I can feel my bones being scrunched.

"It's so nice to see you have arrived here early, dear. I do like punctuality. I must say I am very impressed already young lady," she says in a very refined manner.

Suddenly I feel at ease and start to relax. This results in a big cheeky grin covering my face.

Mrs Evans continues, "Leave your bag down there under my desk, dear. I'll take you for a quick tour around the school and introduce you to some of our residents. After we have finished, Jodie will then show you what she would like you to do today."

I follow Mrs Evans out into the main yard, the smell of horses fills the air. *Mmmm, what a beautiful smell, I just love this smell, a perfect aroma, I wish I could put it in a bottle and carry it around with me all the time.* The sound of hooves on the concrete is music to my ears, and in the distance, I can hear horses whinnying. The yard is already a hive of activity.

"We keep our big horses in this yard dear, twenty-four in total. In the bottom yard, where you'll be helping, we have twenty plus ponies, and another 12 ponies living out," explains Mrs Evans.

For a moment, I have to turn away to hide my smile. I want to giggle every time she calls me 'dear.'

As I look around, wheelbarrows are dotted here and there. Some are full, others only half full and I can hear happy voices chattering away whilst water buckets are filled and feed buckets are washed out. One of the helpers waves to me and I eagerly wave back. I can't help smiling, I'm so happy.

Mrs Evans' walk is a lot faster than mine, so I have to keep jogging to keep up with her. We walk along a big wide concrete path surrounded by beautiful green fields. Two donkeys to the right catch my eye.

Mrs Evans speaks. "The two donkeys you see over there dear, are called Jack and Jill and they came to live here after their elderly owners sadly died. They are inseparable, and are around twenty years of age, which is very young in donkey years. Everyone here absolutely adores them. I'll tell you a very funny story, dear. The daughter of the previous owners told me one day, this was a few years ago mind you, their Great Nan came to stay. She was 81 years old and always loved to sit on a certain wooden bench outside their bungalow reading her daily newspaper. One day the daughter's youngest child, who was only 8 years old, was wandering around holding Jack on a lead rope. The child needed to use the toilet urgently so he decided to tie Jack to the wooden bench where poor Great Nan was sitting. Jill was on her own in the paddock and suddenly she let out an almighty 'Eeyore'. Jack's head shot up in the air. He let out an almighty 'Eeyore' back to her and immediately took off at full speed galloping towards Jill. Unfortunately, Jack was still tied to the wooden bench which he was managing to pull behind him with Great Nan hanging on for dear life!"

I now have a picture of this in my head and cannot stop myself and laugh out loud.

Mrs Evans totally ignores my outburst and continues, "Great Nan did in fact topple off the wooden bench, but thankfully no bones were broken."

I laugh again, this time louder.

Once again Mrs Evans ignores me and continues. "The ponies out in the field on the left live out all year round, dear. They are native breeds so are very tough and hardy. We bring them in every day to check they're all fit and healthy. Sometimes when we have very wet weather, we take them to the indoor school and let them free, dear. They love to run and play, and roll in the sand".

Out of the corner of my eye I suddenly see a very scruffy look-ing pony. She is trotting around proudly with the tip of her tail bone pointing to the sky and her tail flowing out behind her. She turns and prances, then dances, she snorts, and is just generally showing off. My heart is thumping. This is the most beautiful pony I have ever seen in my life.

"Mrs Evans," I blurt out. "What's the name of the pony who is prancing around?"

"That, my dear, is Ballerina. A very sad story. She has been here for about four months now. Janet a friend of mine rescued her. She was on holiday and was out walking her dogs one day and came across this poor mite who had been left all on her own in a field. There wasn't any grass for her to eat, no hay and the water trough only contained dried up mud. She had brambles stuck in her tail and was very weak. To cut a long story short dear, after calling me, my friend managed to track down the owner. She offered him a small amount of money for Ballerina and informed him that if he didn't agree to the deal she would call in the animal welfare. He reluctantly agreed, signed some paper-work and handed over her passport. Janet then called me and I drove to Hampshire with the trailer so we could bring her home. She really was in a pitiful state, very weak and it took us around an hour to get her on her feet and to coax her into the trailer. I called the vets on the way home and they were waiting for us when we arrived back at the yard. Thankfully, my friend had found her just in time. She had worms coming out of her bottom dear, totally dehydrated and she urgently needed to be on a drip to get fluids into her and her teeth needed to be rasped as the poor mite had sores in her mouth. She was also very underweight."

I watch Ballerina, my eyes are full of tears.

"She's beautiful," I quietly mumble.

"I totally agree dear, she's a bit of a handful now though. She has nearly recovered from her terrible ordeal and is proving to be a very strong willed pony. Not many people can get close to her because she likes to take the odd piece of flesh from your body, dear. I need to find time to work with her. The vet thinks she is around five years old, which does match up with the passport."

"I could help you with her," I blurt out from nowhere.

"Maybe in the future dear. Certainly not yet as I don't want you getting hurt," Mrs Evans replies.

Glancing over at Ballerina, I swear she winked at me. I must be imagining things and blink rapidly.

Mrs Evans is walking quickly again. I trot behind her until we eventually arrive at the bottom yard.

The yard is set out in a beautiful big L-shape with a huge hay barn down the bottom of the long end.

It's very impressive. The barn stands tall and wide, and is full to bursting with sweet smelling hay and straw. I take deep breaths inhaling the beautiful aroma and wonder how many bales fit into the barn. Must be hundreds I think to myself.

"This is Orbit," says Mrs Evans in a very fond voice. He's eight years old and as you can see he's a palomino, dear. He's a lovely little mover, sweet natured but also very cheeky. He's a terrible show off and likes to prance around with his tail high in the air, a bit like Ballerina you saw earlier. He's quite a character and a very good jumper."

Moving from stable to stable, she continues to tell me all about the ponies, their ages and how long she has owned them.

There are so many. There's Matty, Sunshine, Trigger, Jet, Snowy, Thimble, St. Christopher, Tinker, Gunner. I stop in my tracks. A beautiful bronze looking pony catches my eye. Mrs Evans informs me his name is Sundance. What a fabulous name. I have a picture in my head of him dancing around in the sun and a big smile covers my face.

I'm finding it very difficult to remember all the names, but much to my relief I notice each pony has a name plate on the front of their stable door. I can't stop thinking about Ballerina. What a beautiful girl she is, and what an awful time she'd had until she was rescued and came to live here.

Mrs Evans now has to rush off to teach a lesson so Jodie takes over and gives me some jobs to do. I'm eager, and can't wait to get started.

Introducing myself to some of the girls, I'm happy to say they are all very friendly and we chat away. One girl in particular, Kate, seems to share my sense of humour and we laugh about various topics as we continue working.

Everybody works really hard and there's no time to stop and have a rest if everything is to be done on time. It is soon lunchtime and Kate asks me if I would like to join her for lunch in the hay barn.

"That would be great, I'll just run and get my sandwiches. I left them in reception earlier."

I return to the barn where Kate is waiting for me, we climb twenty bales high and settle down to have lunch. What a magnificent view of the yard. The smell of horses and ponies, hay and straw fills the air, and I think to myself how heavenly this is. To top it all, I can even see Ballerina happily grazing in the field. I have a warm loving feeling in my heart.

*Here we go,* I silently think to myself as I get out my lunch box.

"Is that Salad Cream I can smell?" asks Kate, sniffing the air looking like a sniffer dog.

"Correct, cucumber, salad cream, covered in lots of black pepper," I reply. "What have you got in yours?"

"Ready salted crisps with Branston pickle on the top," she replies in all seriousness. We fall about laughing and Kate nearly topples off the end of the bale she's sitting on. We're going to get on very well.

"Kate, do you know much about Ballerina? Mrs Evans has told me how her friend rescued her."

"Oh, Ballerina. Yes most people here call her Bella for short."

I interrupt quickly, "Bella, but Bella is going to be the name of my dream pony, when I eventually get her. How spooky is that?"

Kate continues, "I'm not sure this Bella is anyone's dream pony Emily. Only Mrs Evans and Jodie can get near her. She likes to bite people. It's possible someone has hit her over her head at some point because when anyone attempts to stroke her, she pulls her head away so fast and snorts. If you don't move out of the way quickly enough she lunges at you. The lady who rescued her isn't a horsey person, but she couldn't bear to leave her where she was in that desperate state. She does pay for her keep though."

"There's just something about her that I love," I reply. "We have 15 minutes left. I'm going to wander down to see her. Are you coming?"

"You go, I need to wash my hands. I'll see you back in the yard," replies Kate.

I wander down to the field and stand at the wooden post and rail gently calling to Bella. Lifting her head Bella looks straight at me. She takes a few steps towards me then stops. I continue to talk to her in a gentle voice. She comes another step nearer and puts her head high in the air and snorts. I turn my head slightly away from her. My heart is pounding, she is so beautiful. Her coat is a dirty cream colour and I sigh. The vision I have of my dream pony, is that she will be a golden dun in colour.

"Bella, come nearer to me. I'm not going to hurt you," I say in a gentle voice. My head is still turned away from her, I continue, "You are the most beautiful girl I have ever seen in the whole of my life." I stoop down low. Bella is now only two feet away. I'm as still as a statue. She's coming nearer. She puts her head over the fence to smell my hair. I can smell and feel her warm breath blowing gently on my head. I'm literally glued to the spot. Bella moves backwards, snorts and trots away. I'm grinning like a Cheshire cat.

My first day is amazing. I carry so many water buckets, my arms feel as if they're going to drop off. Suddenly, I have a vision of arriving home a couple of inches shorter and dragging my hands along the ground, like an orang-utan because my arms have stretched so much with the heavy lifting. Mum's face would be a picture. I can't help myself and burst out laughing.

I've lifted countless bales of hay and straw onto wheelbarrows, and to be honest I've lost count of how many times I went from the hay barn to the stables and back again. I now know how a Yoyo feels. I hosed down the main yard and now have blisters on my hands from so much sweeping.

I'm completely shattered at the end of my shift, and after saying my goodbyes and blowing a kiss to Bella, I very slowly cycle home. My arms ache, my legs ache, my back aches and I feel as if I have been thrown through a hedge.

Mum and Dad are waiting for me when I get in. They are eager to hear about my first day.

"Well? How did it go love?" asks Mum.

I tell them about the donkeys and of course, all about Bella. Mum has tears in her eyes as she listens, and blurts out, "How can people be so evil to an innocent animal?"

Dad being Dad tells me to be very careful and to listen to Mrs Evans. He doesn't want me getting hurt or bitten.

At last, it's time for a nice long bath to help ease my aching bones and to change into something nice and comfortable.

It's all I can do to eat my dinner. My eyes are very heavy and start to close. I'm so very tired.

Excusing myself from the table I hobble to my bedroom with every intention of reading some chapters of my latest book before I go to sleep. I crawl into bed and open my book….

I open my eyes and blink rapidly, the light is shining in through a gap in my curtains. My book is still open at the same page and more or less in the same place on the bed. I must have been totally exhausted and fallen asleep as soon as my head hit the pillow, hardly moving at all during the night.

# Chapter 4

* * *

OVER THE LAST FEW MONTHS, I've become an expert at mucking out, sweeping yards and grooming. Mrs Evans has very high standards. She cannot abide even the smallest piece of straw being left on the yard, so if I have to get on my hands and knees to pick up any stray pieces, that is exactly what I do.

Most importantly, I've been doing really well with Bella. I had a slight set back on week three though. I'd been standing chatting to her over the fence, when suddenly with no warning at all, she lunged at me biting me very hard on the top of my arm. I automatically jumped back, but her teeth pinched my skin deeply and it really did hurt. I had to inform Mrs Evans because the skin was broken. She tutted at me, cleaned my wound and told me I must listen to her in future. I apologised to her, and she nodded. Dad, well as you can imagine, was not happy. He argued with me about going back, especially when the enormous black and blue bruise appeared covering most of my top arm. Thankfully, Mum had a quiet chat with him and he didn't mention the incident again.

Grooming the ponies is definitely my favourite task. I find it very relaxing and therapeutic. Some of the horses and ponies even love to have a massage.

Mrs Evans, according to Jodie, is very pleased with my work. I try my best and do work very hard. I also have fun with my new friends, both the human variety and the horses and ponies.

I help Jodie make up the feeds, and the smell of garlic fills the air. There are so many different types of feed: bran, oats, barley, nuts, pasture mix, chaff and lots of additives like garlic, honey, cider vinegar, vitamins, herbs, cod liver oil - the list is endless. Some of the ponies have the same food, and others have completely different diets depending on their needs. Every pony has their own menu for morning and evening written on a wipe board. This makes it quite easy to follow, but it does take a while to mix them all up. I've lost count of how many feed buckets I've washed out. Must be hundreds possibly even thousands.

The time has flown by and it's now eleven months and two weeks since I first started at the riding school.

"Emily dear, please come and see me in my office at 3.00pm will you?" Mrs Evans calls out to me as I sweep the yard.

I raise my hand in acknowledgement, but my heart is sinking. I really cannot think of anything I've done wrong and more worryingly, I've never been summoned to the office before.

At 2.55pm I nervously make my way to the office. As I reach the door I take a deep breath, raise my right hand and knock twice. I listen intently but not hearing anything, I slowly open the door, just enough to peer around into the room.

Mrs Evans is sitting at her desk, her glasses perched on the end of her nose. She lifts her head up as I open the door. "My dear Emily, do come in and sit down, dear," she is smiling at me and indicates for me to sit on the chair opposite.

Gulping, I enter the room and close the door quietly behind me. Two 'dears' in once sentence, I think this must be serious. Normally this would have struck me as funny, but at this present moment I'm too nervous to think straight.

Mrs Evans waits for me to sit down and continues, "Emily dear, we are so pleased with your work over the last year. You've been an asset to our school. You're a very popular girl and liked by everyone here. Jodie and I now feel it's time for you to learn to ride, if you would like to of course, dear?"

*Like to!* I wasn't expecting this and can't help but screech, "Yes, please!" But in a split second, I think about what she has just said, and sit quietly. I'm thinking hard.

"What's wrong, dear?" enquires Mrs Evans obviously puzzled by my serious expression.

"Mrs Evans, how much will this cost? I'm saving so hard to buy my own pony, I'm not really sure I can afford to have riding lessons."

"Don't be silly, dear. I'm not expecting you to pay for the lessons. You've worked so hard and as a thank you, I feel in return it's now time for me to teach you to ride. This is the next step forward for you. I've also noticed that you have been doing very well with Bella. I've watched you at lunchtimes, and I'm totally amazed that you can stroke her all over her head, and shoulders and she hasn't bit you since that early incident. I would like you to help me with her, would that be ok with you?"

*"Awesome, Mrs Evans,"* I think to myself, but accidently say it out loud.

Mrs Evans just smiles and nods her head.

Today is the day, my first riding lesson. This is the day I've been wait-ing for. Jodie asks me to 'tack up' Matty, and to make sure I'm ready to meet Mrs Evans in the indoor school at 2.00pm sharp.

I adore Matty, he's really sweet. At 18 years old, he is always used to teach the beginners. I chat softly to him as I groom him, the brush smoothly flowing over his beautiful coat. I quietly ask him to be a good boy for me today. The grooming is now finished, I place the brushes back in their box, untie him and together we walk towards the school. I wave to Bella on the way, and she whinnies as I call her name. My heart as usual is filled with joy and love for her.

Mrs Evans is waiting for me and talks me through how to mount a pony properly.

"Now Emily, dear, bring Matty over here to the mounting block, that's right. As you progress you will be able to get on board without using the block if you prefer, but to begin with I think we should use it. Now, I will hold Matty for you beside the mounting block while you climb the few steps, and stand on the top ready to mount. Good. Now, gather the reins up in your left hand, you can hold onto a piece of his mane too if it makes you feel more secure. Place your left foot in the stirrup and swing your right leg over Matty's back. Try and lower yourself down gently onto his back. It's not very nice for him to have someone thump down onto him."

Trying very hard to do exactly as Mrs Evans was instructing, amazingly, a few seconds later I'm sitting nicely in the saddle on his back. This is just awesome.

"Good girl. Nicely done, dear," Mrs Evans praises. "Now, I'll lead you around and you just sit there and get used to the feel of it and concentrate on your balance."

My lesson lasts 40 minutes and I have learnt so much. How to sit nicely in the saddle, keep my back straight, look ahead and to keep my hands very soft on the reins. I thoroughly enjoy every second of my first lesson and the time has flown by all too quickly.

"Emily I have to go now, but I want to say a very well done, dear. You are a natural in the saddle," says Mrs Evans. Once again, I grin like a Cheshire cat.

I ride Matty out of the school and back to his stable. I slip both of my feet out of the stirrups and dismount. I give him an extra big hug, untack him and thank him for being a good boy for me.

My next port of call is to skip down the path to tell Bella all about my first lesson. She sees me coming, whinnies and trots straight over to me. I chat away and tell her everything I have been doing, her ears move around until eventually she lets out a huge yawn.

"Oh Bella, I'm so sorry. Am I boring you?" Bella's response is to snort, turn around and walk away. What a comical pony she is. The very first time I saw Bella, she was a mucky cream in colour and then in March she turned chocolate in colour. In May I couldn't believe my eyes as I watched her coat change again, this time into a shiny golden colour. Could Bella be my dream pony after all?

# Chapter 5

* * *

IT'S ONLY BEEN FIVE WEEKS since my first riding lesson, and I can already do a rising trot to perfection. I'm progressing to a canter and I'm now riding Gunner. At 12 years old, he's a lot faster than good old Matty.

I really do love the speed. It gives me such a thrill.

Mrs Evans is working with Bella, and I'm helping. To everyone's utter amazement I can actually groom her now. Every time I'm at the riding school, and my chores are finished, I rush off to see Bella. She always comes straight to me, I put her head collar on, and we walk to the stable. Whilst grooming her I tell her everything I've been up to. Most of the time she listens patiently, but I still have to keep a close eye on her and stay alert. If I'm relaxed, Bella is relaxed. Mrs Evans has taught me how to recognise the signs Bella shows when she has had enough. If she starts getting fidgety, I stop. I've read many books on body language and about rescue ponies. Maybe one day I could run my own rescue sanctuary. How wonderful would that be?

Mrs Evans is really working hard with Bella. She is lunging her in the school at least three times a week and Bella has even had a saddle on. To everyone's surprise she didn't even object. Mrs Evans feels one hundred per cent positive that Bella was a family pony at some time in her early life, was probably outgrown and moved on eventually but sadly fell into the wrong hands. This really breaks my heart, but sadly happens so often in the world we live in today. I feel very sad but going through all of this with Bella has given me passion and fire in my heart to know I want to help as many animals as I possibly can when I'm older. I've built a very special bond with Bella. I just can't explain the feeling. We understand each other and what I feel for her I am assuming is true love.

I continue to arrive even earlier than normal at the riding school, always trotting down the path to spend time with Bella first. She whinnies and trots towards me, drops her head over the fence for me to stroke her. She loves to have her ears rubbed and my heart is overfilled with love for her. What a different pony she now is, the old saying that 'time is a great healer' is true. She has learnt to trust again and to realise not all humans are bad. I stay late after I've finished my work so Bella and I can spend even more quality time together.

I've had a few falls whilst riding, but to be honest these never bother me. I just get up, brush myself down and get back on again! I don't tell Dad too much as he would give me a lecture but I do confide in Mum.

Four weeks ago, I sprained my wrist when Rocky, a big black horse, barged past me in the stable, pushing me hard up against the wall. My wrist had to be bandaged for two weeks but I managed to carry on with my work at the riding school. I couldn't hide this from Dad but to my amazement he was very cool about it, and I didn't receive a lecture. Phew! I did try to tell Mum I couldn't wash up for a week, but she wasn't having any of that saying, "Emily, if you're ok to go to the riding school, then I'm sure you can manage to wash up!" Fair comment but well worth a try!

I'm now riding Orbit, and doing really well, even if I do say so myself. My confidence is soaring and I'm so happy. I've also learnt how to jump. Wow, I love jumping, it is a totally awesome feeling. Orbit and I make a great team. We have taken part in so many things,

 including a charity fancy dress ride through the village. This was to help raise money for repairs to the village hall. I had dressed up as an Indian girl and Kate dressed up as a cow girl. We all had so much fun planning this day.

In total twenty two ponies and riders took part and we raised an amazing £845.00. Mrs Evans was extremely proud of all of us. I do have to say she was absolutely glowing on the day, possibly due the local press and the Mayor being in attendance. She was in her element! (Her lipstick had also been perfect for the photographs, I'd noticed!).

One Saturday, the biggest horse at the school, Banjo, a solidly built Shire horse 17.2 hands high, stood on my foot. I'd been unable to move at all as he was so heavy and I had to shout for assistance. Jodie came rushing over to help move him off. This left a very large hoof print on my boot and a badly bruised my foot. My toes went black and eight weeks later, can you believe it, my big toe nail fell off! YUK! I wasn't too worried though. On the positive side, one less toe nail to paint!

I have truly learnt so much. How to pick out hooves making sure they are nice and clean, tacking up horses, putting their rugs on and taking them off, how to soak hay for those with allergies, putting 'brushing boots' on, the list is endless. I'm excellent at cleaning tack now as Jodie makes sure I have plenty of practice!

I also help with worming the horses and know how to treat small wounds and injuries. Whenever the vet is around at the weekends, I always offer to be his assistant. I'm not squeamish at all, and have watched him closely as he's stitched wounds, applied poultices to treat abscesses, take temperatures, and rasp teeth.

I really enjoy the veterinary side, and make notes so I can read them over and over again when I get home. Maybe I could study to become a vet when I leave school?

I'm amazed as each day I still continue to learn new things. Today, Mrs Evans asks me to get Bella ready and bring her into the school. "Fully tack her up, dear, and I'll meet you in half an hour."

I get Bella ready and we walk over to the school. Mrs Evans takes her from me and instructs me to go and get my riding hat. I'm totally confused, but do as she asks. I sit and watch as Mrs Evans lunges Bella for twenty minutes. I love this pony so much; she makes my heart jump every time I look at her and even more so when she looks at me.

Jodie pops her head in, and Mrs Evans calls her over. "Right Emily, dear. Jodie is going to gently leg you up onto Bella so that you're just leaning over her. Jodie will keep hold of you. Is this ok?"

I stand with my jaw wide open. *'Did I hear right? Am I really going to sit on Bella'?*

"Chop, chop, dear," Mrs Evans' voice brings me back to reality.

Slowly I take a deep breath and walk over to Bella and stroke her beautiful soft neck, talking gently to her. I place my hands onto her withers and lift my left leg so Jodie can gently push me up until I am leaning over Bella's back. Bella doesn't move an inch and after two minutes Mrs Evans asks me to lever myself up and put my right leg over the saddle until I am sitting upright. This is the most amazing moment of my life. Mrs Evans slowly leads Bella forward. I sit relaxed, take deep breaths and stay as calm as possible in the saddle.

Bella jumps slightly to the right but apart from this walks around beautifully as I continue to talk to her in a very soft voice. We continue like this for fifteen minutes, I want to stay on her forever. Mrs Evans thinks we have done enough for today.

I dismount and throw my arms around Bella, out of the corner of my eye I can see Mrs Evans beaming. "Well done, dear" she praises.

Bella still doesn't like or trust certain people, not many of the helpers want to have anything to do with her. I find this very odd. She is the most beautiful pony in the whole world, well to me anyway!

Every weekend and a couple of evenings after school I continue to ride Bella in the school and we have progressed to trotting and recently cantering. I still have my riding lesson every Sunday at two o'clock and I've now ridden nearly every horse and pony at the school. I'm really very proud as I'm the only one who rides Bella.

It's now eighteen months since I started at the Riding School, and I haven't missed a single weekend. When I had a nasty cold and my limbs felt like they were falling off, when I sprained my wrist in the stable, when I sprained my ankle in a school hockey match, when my toe nail fell off, when there was three inches of snow on the ground, when there was black ice everywhere, I still turned up.

I recently heard Mum talking to Nan H on the telephone, telling her with no doubt at all, I had certainly proved what a tough and determined young lady I have grown into and how very proud she is of me. A huge smile emerged across my face.

# Chapter 6

* * *

IT REALLY IS UNBELIEVABLE HOW time flies. I now know where the saying comes from, 'time flies when you are having fun.' It's been twenty-one months since I started helping at the riding school. I've had such fun and learnt so much.

I think it's now time to ask Mum and Dad that very important question again. This is the moment I've been working towards.

I think they have an idea of what's coming. With a nice glass of strawberry milkshake and not forgetting my favourite chocolate digestives, we all sit around the kitchen table.

"Mum, Dad," I begin, looking at each of them in turn.

"Yes, Emily, love," says Mum smiling at me.

"In just over three months I will be fifteen. Do you think it's possible for me to have a pony of my own now? Maybe in time for my birthday please? With my paper round and pocket money, I've saved over £900 and I will still continue to earn money weekly. What do you think?' I hold my breath.

Mum and Dad look at each other. Then they smile, and Dad is the first to speak.

"Well, Emily, we are so very proud of what you've achieved and yes, Mum and I agree that you are now ready to own your own pony."

These are the words I've been waiting to hear for so many years. I can't help but let out a huge scream of delight.

"Hold on, Emily," said Dad. "We need to talk this through with Mrs Evans first. If she agrees with us, and thinks you're ready, we will have to make a start converting the old barn into a stable and tack room.

My jaw is wide open, and I can feel my eyes nearly popping out of my head. I just sit and stare at Dad.

Dad continues, "We've been thinking about this for quite a while now. The barn looks very run down and tired so by sprucing it up, well this will add value to the property too. We're sure we can get help from family and friends, and converting it shouldn't be too costly because the main structure is already in place and sound. I can get the materials directly from the wholesaler, and Jack, (Dads best friend) should be able to lay the concrete. We can add some post and rail fencing around the two-acre field and then divide it into two. We'll also need you to help as much as you can with the labour. So, what do you think?" he asks with a big grin on his face.

For a moment, I'm speechless, I spring off my chair and run around the table to give Dad a big hug and then Mum. "I love you, I love you. You're the best Mum and Dad in the whole world." Tears are streaming down my face and I am on cloud nine. My mind is racing. The second paddock will be right outside my bedroom window. How awesome is this?

"We'll try as hard as we can to get it ready for your birthday, Emily, we'll do our best, I promise."

The following day we all head off to see Mrs Evans.

"Good afternoon, come on in, my dears," she greets us in a very warm manner.

I smile, as over the last twenty one months, I've grown very fond of her calling me 'dear'. Mum and Dad explain everything, and thankfully Mrs Evans agrees. She says she has no doubts at all, and feels I'm more than ready, and very capable of looking after a pony of my own.

As I hear these words I want to throw my arms around her and hug her, but I just about refrain from doing so. She also agrees to help us look for a suitable pony.

For a moment, I feel really bad. "Mrs Evans," I begin and take a gulp.

"Yes, Emily. What is it, dear?" she asks smiling directly at me.

"Mrs Evans, I really appreciate all the help you've given me, and you've taught me so much. I'll always be so grateful to you, but once I have my own pony, I won't be able to help you anymore at the weekends. I'll really miss you all, and I feel really sad."

Mrs Evans smiles and looks directly at me, "Emily, dear, I will be very sad to lose you too. You're a very big part of our team here, but I fully understand. Of course when you have your own pony, he or she will be your main priority. Please don't forget dear, you will always be very welcome to come over here any time you want to."

"Thank you," I just about manage to blurt out. There is a huge lump in my throat. Pulling myself together quicker than a pair of curtains, I babble out, "Mrs Evans, do you think Janet would sell Bella to me. I really do love her?"

Mum and Dad turn to stare at me. They are obviously very surprised at this request.

"Well dear, I can ask her, but unfortunately she's in Thailand for 3 months helping at a Dog Rescue Sanctuary, I am not sure I'll be able to make contact with her. I will certainly try and tell her how amazing you are with Bella. I will also tell her we are never going to be able to use Bella in the riding school due to her temperament. I promise I will email her and also text her, dear. Leave it with me?" I grin at her.

"Do you think Bella is the right pony for Emily," Dad blurts out aimed directly at Mrs Evans.

"Emily has an amazing connection with Bella. I'm also happy to continue working with both of them, but I'm not sure if Janet will want to sell her. When she rescued Bella, she did say she would never let her leave the school. I will definitely ask and put Emily's case forward though. That is all I can do."

My face suddenly drops and I'm feeling very emotional. I love Bella and want her to be mine, all mine.

I can feel the tears slowly running down my cheeks and I excuse myself quickly leaving Mum and Dad with Mrs Evans and I rush out to the yard looking for Kate, wiping my tears away as I go. I tell Kate about everything that has just happened and she gives me a big hug. She truly is a great friend and I feel very lucky to have met her. She is going to cross all of her fingers and toes that Mrs Evans can get hold of Janet and also that she agrees to sell Bella to me.

It turns out that Kate won't be at the riding school in a couple of months either. Her dad has been offered a job transfer and the family are moving to Norwich. I'm pleased for Kate and her family. I will miss her terribly. We'll skype and call each other regularly and we have promised to keep in touch on Facebook. I give her a big hug and rush back to Mrs Evan's office.

# Chapter 7

* * *

It's now the last week of May. We have been really busy organising everything. The wood panels are here, and it is now feeling very real. I cannot tell you how excited I am.

Uncle Gary is coming in the evenings and at the weekends. Jack together with two other strong friends, are also helping evenings and weekends, and we mustn't forget my Dad. Uncle Gary has to sort out the water supply first, followed by the electrics and bless him, he's been very busy the last three evenings.

I help as much as I can, trying not to get in anyone's way at the same time. I'm having a great time and learning so many new things.

I love my Uncle Gary. He's so funny, always telling me silly jokes and making me laugh. He teases me a lot too.

Words cannot tell you how relieved I was that I had to work last weekend. They were clearing the barn of all the junk and the spiders. Oh, those spiders. I shiver at the thought.

It's now time for the internal boards to go up. They're going all around the inside of the barn.

I am standing and staring at this huge box. It looks to contain hundreds, maybe thousands of nails. Surely it is going to take me days, maybe weeks to hammer this lot in? I know it will be worth it in the end so I had better get cracking. My hands are aching from all of the hammering and at last the final piece of kickboard is up. I take a step back to look at my handy work, let out a huge sigh of contentment and a smile of relief. Everything is starting to take shape. My tummy feels like it has hundreds of butterflies flying around inside.

Jack is in charge of driving the digger. I did tell him I would be happy to give it a go myself, but he politely declined. I watch eagerly as Jack digs out the base in the barn, plus an area of around twelve feet at the front. The soil he's dug out now needs moving, and this seriously takes me hours. I shovel soil into wheelbarrow after wheelbarrow, I wheel each barrow to the wooded area, and tip it out. I never imagined soil could be so heavy. My arms ache, the sweat pours from my brow and I continue to do this for the next three days. It seems like an eternity.

Twice the wheelbarrow falls over half way down to the wooded area, and twice I nearly swear.

Finally, the last wheelbarrow load is tipped. Eureka!

I'm surplus to requirements for the next two evenings as the hard core needs to be put down, followed by a membrane to damp proof it. I can't tell you how relieved I am. My poor body is in need of some recovery time. Again, my arms feel like those of an Orang-utan.

I offer to be on tea duty and wish I hadn't as this turns out to be more tiring than I had anticipated. I continuously run in and out, I feel like a Yoyo again, and forget who is having tea, and who is having coffee. I am under pressure, I run to fetch my notepad from my bedroom to write it all down but as normal I'm in such a hurry, miss my footing on the kitchen step, and bang, I trip and land on my rump before I can stop myself. Very painful, but a short sharp lesson to slow down. I seriously can't wait until bed time, I'm exhausted.

I've been taking photos of all the different stages of the building work, and have downloaded them to my computer. I've sent some of the photo's to Kate, and also to Sophie. They both seem to be as excited as I am.

I stand and gaze through my bedroom window, I can't believe the transformation. My dream is actually starting to come true. This is going to be my pony's stable and tack room, together with the paddock, and I can see all of this from my bedroom window.

Uncle Gary shouts out to me bringing me back to reality from my day dream. "Emily, get that kettle boiling, move it, groove it girl." I burst out laughing and go and do just that.

The concrete is due to arrive soon, and Dad and Jack are ready and waiting. Apparently this is the hardest part of the conversion because they're going to be working against the clock, laying and levelling the concrete before it dries.

We've all prayed for a dry day, and thankfully we're in luck. It's cloudy, but dry and warm, although the temperature is due to climb this afternoon. The workers sweat as wheelbarrow after wheelbarrow of concrete is taken to the barn. They work as fast as they can, and I feel sorry that I can't help with this part.

"The kettle's on, and I've got you all a special treat of chocolate biscuits," I shout to them.

Two days later, more concrete arrives. This is for the front of the barn. Two more packets of chocolate digestives gone but they all deserve it. I'm buying the refreshments out of my own money, I feel this is the least I can do. Time for me to cycle to the local shop and restock.

It's now Saturday, and today I am once again relieved to be working at the riding school. Whilst I'm away, Jack, Uncle Gary and Dad are in charge of putting the partition through the middle of the barn, fit the stable door, and tack room door.

I've thoroughly enjoyed today. After helping to look after the horses in the morning, I spend an hour chatting and grooming Bella. Sadly there is still no news from Janet. Mrs Evans told me her emails are bouncing back, and Janet isn't due home until September. I sigh with disappointment.

It's seven o'clock, I arrive home and work is still in progress so once again I offer to be on tea duty again. Eventually the sunlight is starting to disappear, and we have to stop. It's been a long day and everyone is totally exhausted.

I can't wait to have a proper look at everything in the morning in daylight.

✳  ✳  ✳

Argh! 6.00am, the alarm is beeping at me again. Today is Sunday. I jump out of bed, grab my camera, and as quiet as a mouse let myself out of the bungalow. I'm so impatient to see how everything is looking in the yard. Still in my PJ's, I run across to the barn for a sneaky look. I wish I'd remembered to put on some shoes, or slippers. *OUCH!*

I'm not disappointed. In fact I'm thrilled. This is awesome, actually beyond my wildest dreams. I can't believe I'm looking at what used to be the old spooky barn I was so scared of. It is new, bright and seems to be smiling at me. This is a very happy building. I grin from ear to ear like a Cheshire cat.

The icing on the cake would be to have Bella standing here with me too.

I glance at my watch, 6.25am, time for me to get back. Skipping across the lush green grass to the side, to avoid hurting my feet again, I hurry back indoors, wash and dress in record time, dash back outside, grab my bike, and head off on my paper round.

I could be imagining it, but this morning I swear the birds are singing louder than normal, and such beautiful tunes. I'm sure they're feeling my happiness.

7.45am and I am back home. Everyone has arrived, and Mum looks in her element cooking a nice breakfast. The smell of sizzling bacon and Quorn sausages fills the air, laughter fills the room, and I stand and grin my cheeks off again!

"Morning all," I shout as I make my way through the kitchen.

The plan today, is to put in the post and rail fencing around the yard area. Uncle Gary's job is to sort out where the outside water tap is going. Jack is going to cut out an arc for a window to provide ventilation. His two friends, who look as though they're thoroughly enjoying Mum's breakfast, are doing the fencing around the paddock. I have offered to take the day off from the riding school to help, but to my relief Dad says he has enough help.

By the time I arrive home at seven o'clock, the last rail has just been hammered on. It's nearly finished. Everyone gathers up their belongings and shout their goodbye's as they leave. I thank them all again and give Uncle Gary an extra big hug. I am sure they can't wait to get home, have a shower, and put their feet up.

After my paper round today and before I go to school, my task is to sweep out what use to be the old barn. I complete my paper round in record time, and I am now standing here looking around in admiration. I feel I need to pinch myself, it still doesn't seem real.

Today is the 21st of July. The stable and tack room are finished, and a lovely concrete yard stands glistening in the sunshine to the front of the old barn. Turning on the water tap I watch the water gush out, this is awesome.

I test the portable lights in the stable and tack room. On, off, on, off. Wow! Dad has managed to fit these with the help of Uncle Gary, and they have also added a big security light to the front of the stable.

Having watched this from day one, again I can't quite believe my dream is actually becoming a reality.

Yesterday, Mr Newman, the local farmer who lives down the lane, arrived with his tractor, and delivered 30 bales of straw and 15 bales of hay. These are stacked behind the barn under large tarpaulin sheets.

I just adore the smell of the hay. I had slowly stacked bale after bale and just for a minute it smelt so good, I really wanted to eat some myself. I decided against it and instead I walked around with one strand of hay hanging from my mouth. Soon, I hope and I prayer, I will be making a nice straw bed for my very own pony. Will it be Bella?

It is now 4.00pm and Nan and Grandad D are due to arrive for dinner. I can see their car arriving and trot across to welcome them. I haven't seen them for well over three weeks. I grab each one by their arm and drag them towards the newly converted old barn. They are gobsmacked and can't believe it's the same building.

"This looks wonderful, Emily, dear. Your Mum has told me how hard you've been working and your Grandad and I are truly very proud of you," Nan whispers to me giving me a massive hug at the same time. I grin.

"Emily, come back to the car with us, we have something for you," says Grandad.

On the back seat of their estate car, is a wheelbarrow, a pitchfork, a shovel, a broom, a hosepipe and three plastic feed bins. I can't believe my eyes. Nan continues, 'These are your early birthday presents Emily, and part of your Christmas present too."

"Thank you Nan and Grandad. You are truly wonderful."

Dad helps me unload the items from the car. We pile most of them into the wheelbarrow, but only manage to fit in one of the feed bins, together with the other items. I wheel these to the tack room, with dad following along behind with the other two feed bins.

We place my new items in their allocated spaces, I stand and stare, not quite believing what I'm seeing. I'm so happy. This has saved me so much money. They are all on the list of items I need to buy.

The following day Nan and Grandad H arrive. I have only just got in from school. Only two days left, and the summer holidays begin. I've been counting the days.

Nan and Grandad have also brought my birthday presents over early and carry them into the bungalow. They insist I open them now. I'm more than a little confused as it's not my birthday just yet, but if it makes them happy, then I'd better get cracking.

I sit down and unwrap my gifts and find a beautiful red lead rope (this will match my head collar that has been in my wardrobe for months), a lunge whip and a lunge rein. Nan asks me to look behind the sofa, I oblige and I am really surprised to see a sack of nuts, a sack of chaff and pasture mix plus a hay rack for the stable. This is fantastic, but how do they all know these items are on my list? Suddenly, it all falls into place. Mum has been peeping at my list.

"Thanks Mum," I say as I turn and grin at her. She grins back and winks at me. Now time for me to give big hugs all around and thank my Nan and Grandad once again.

# Chapter 8

* * *

I'VE BEEN COUNTING DOWN THE days, at last it's the twenty fourth of July. Today is the last day of school and more importantly the start of a long summer holiday.

Thankfully it is nearly the end of the last lesson of today and the buzzer goes off which is music to my ears. The last class of term is now over. I throw my arms up in the air and shout "Yippee" as I eagerly cram everything into my school bag as quickly as I can and rush to say goodbye to my friends. Today, I need to get home fast.

Aunty Lynette, cousins Sophie, eleven years old, and Amy, nine years old, are popping over. I'm really looking forward to showing them my stable. Both girls ride, but neither have their own pony yet.

Sophie and I regularly email each other, or chat on Facebook. We are very close, get on really well and we have so much in common.

4.30pm, and Aunty Lynette promptly arrives carrying two carrier bags of presents. She gives me a huge hug. "Open them up," she urges. "We want you to have them now. You may get your pony before your birthday and to be honest we are almost as excited as you are."

I eagerly open the presents one by one, Amy is sitting next to me. Sophie is perched on a chair close by. Both their faces are gleaming with pure excitement. I'm so thrilled. More items to cross off my wish list. First aid box, bandages, cotton wool, poultice pads, antiseptic cream, and a tin of hoof oil with a brush. I give each of the girls and my aunty a big hug and thank them for my wonderful presents, I grab each of my cousins by the hand, and the three of us run outside to the stable.

"Wow," screeches Sophie. "This is just amazing."

They absolutely love it, and can't believe the transformation.

"Come on, let's go and sit down and have a catch up," I suggest.

We chat away sitting in the glorious sunshine, talking about ponies and adventures and we are so happy and thrilled because we have no more school for seven weeks. More importantly no more homework.

It is now the day after and Uncle Gary arrives with my cousins, Chris, Martin, and their two rescue dogs, Bailey and Millie. Chris and Martin are identical twins, eleven years old and like their Dad, have a wonderful sense of humour.

It is truly wonderful and I am so happy that all of my family absolutely adore all animals.

Bailey and Millie are such well-behaved dogs. They sit nicely and look up at me, both holding out a paw. I bend down to shake their paws in greeting, and try not to laugh at them. "Hi you handsome boy Bailey, hello pretty Millie," I say as I stoop down low. I'm rewarded with a sloppy kiss from each of them. We all burst out laughing, and Bailey looks me straight in the eyes and lets out a big "Woof!"

Uncle Gary says, "Aunty Sharon sadly can't come today as she's working. Although she sends her love and big hugs to you and will definitely pop by to see you before your birthday." Aunty Sharon is a nurse at the local hospital, she is such a lovely, caring person.

"I have my instructions from your Aunty, we are here to deliver your birthday presents. We've heard a rumour, something about you might be getting a nag," laughs Uncle Gary. Martin tuts at his Dad in a comical way, and Chris just laughs. "Come on, Emily," Uncle Gary urges, "Hurry up and open your presents, I am eager to show the boys my superb handy work."

Bailey, and Millie, decide they're going to help me open my presents, I hold one end, and they grab the other end. Bailey let's go and is now running off with an envelope in his mouth. I call him over, ask him to sit and to drop. He immediately obliges and is now sitting patiently with his eyes totally focussed on the envelope. It's a gift voucher to use at my local saddlery to buy the bridle of my choice. *Wow!*

In the meantime, Millie has been busy opening one of my other presents. She's managed this without any help, I turn to look at her and can see she has her head inside a water bucket and I hear something rattling inside. Investigating I can see a smaller present at the bottom of the bucket. Millie eventually turns the water bucket upside down, and the present falls out onto the floor. Bailey eagerly pinches it from under her nose, and runs off with Millie chasing behind. How I love these two dogs.

Chris eventually retrieves the present, which is now totally unwrapped and hands it to me. A marker pen. I look at him with a puzzled expression. They all laugh and Uncle Gary explains, "You have a wipe board in the van, but it's far too big to wrap. Give me a tool kit, and I'm happy. Ask me to wrap something, well, I haven't got a clue," he laughs heartily.

"Come on you bunch, let's go and see where this old nag is going to live," laughs Uncle Gary, winking at me. We all troop out to the old barn with the two dogs, who of course, race ahead and get there a lot faster than we do.

"Not bad old boy," chides Martin looking at his father. "Didn't know you had it in you," he laughs heartily as he runs away with Uncle Gary giving chase, calling Martin a cheeky so and so as he goes. Uncle Gary eventually catches up with Martin, grabs him by his belt, and turns him upside down until he apologises.

Watching the commotion, Bailey runs over and continuously licks Martin's upside down face, which makes him wriggle even more. We're all in fits of laughter.

The morning flies by far too quickly, and before long, it's time for them to leave. I thank them all again, and they climb into their van to head back home. My face seriously aches from laughing so much.

"Emily, you have a letter in the kitchen," Mum shouts to me. I run into the kitchen and eagerly grab the envelope from the table where Mum has left it. It's from a pony magazine I buy regularly.

Opening it as fast as I can, I read, "We are very pleased to inform you Emily, you have come second in our poetry competition. Your entry will be published in next month's edition. Enclosed is a £25.00 voucher for you to use at a saddlery of your choice. Congratulations, and thank you for participating."

How I had completely forgotten about entering, I do not know, and hearing my squeals of delight, Mum comes running into the kitchen wondering what on earth is happening. I'd also forgotten to tell her and Dad that I had entered the competition, what with so many other things happening. Handing the letter to Mum, she clears her throat, and reads out my poem.

*One day I will own a pony, she will be a golden dun*
*We will ride together everywhere, and have, oh so much fun*

*Over the Downs we will gallop, the wind blowing through her mane*
*Through the woods, through the trees, in sunshine and in rain.*
*I will call my pony Bella, she will be, my best friend,*
*Every Christmas and on birthdays, a card to her I'll send.*
*I will lose my heart to my pony, when eventually my dream comes true*
*And I promise that every day and night, I will tell her, I love you.*

Mum wipes what looks like a tear from her eye and gives me a big hug. "Well done, love," she whispers.

It's now late evening, I'm in my bedroom going through my wish list. I can't believe it. I only have two items left to get. A saddle, and most importantly, my pony. Will it be Bella?

Once again, I gallop down the hallway, accompanied by my whip, and into the lounge to tell Mum and Dad. This time I don't fall over and scare the wits out of them.

Mum suggests, "How about asking the family to give you money for Christmas this year? You also have your £25.00 voucher from your poetry competition, and Dad and I will give you £80.00 for an early Christmas gift. We're happy to lend you the money to buy the saddle when you need it, and you can pay us back later."

"All you need to worry about then, is finding your pony," Dad adds glancing up from reading his newspaper.

"Whoopee!" I scream, and dance around the lounge. "Thank you, oh thank you!"

All that remains now is, "MY PONY." Will it be Bella?

# Chapter 9

## * * *

A WEEK HAS GONE BY and I am gutted as there is still no news from Janet. Mrs Evans has taken us to see many ponies for sale, Dad has taken certain days off work to come along with us, but unfortunately Mum couldn't get any time off work. I go along with all of this because I know they are only trying to help, but the only pony I truly want is Bella.

Up until now, we haven't found a single pony that I've fallen in love with. I've truly lost my heart to Bella.

It's now the 6th August, two days before my birthday, and Janet still hasn't responded to Mrs Evans' numerous emails and texts.

Beep, beep. "Are you ready?" Mrs Evans shouts from her land rover. We're going to visit a friend of hers who has two ponies that she feels may be suitable. Sadly, neither are what I'm looking for. I only want Bella. We climb back into her car and head for home. I stare out of the car window, tears run slowly down my cheeks. Why isn't Janet answering Mrs Evans emails and texts?

Two hours later and we're nearly home. "Emily, dear, would you like to come back to the school with me?" Mrs Evans asks. "Yes please," I reply. I really want to spend some time with Bella. "Can I call Mum and Dad to let them know when we get back to the school?" "Of course you can, dear", she responds.

Jumping out of the land rover, I thank Mrs Evans, rush to the office to call Mum and Dad and I am now at last feeling happy again as I skip down the path to see Bella. Her ears prick up as she sees me, she whinnies and canters straight across to me. I open the gate to the field and Bella comes closer. I can feel her soft velvet muzzle on my cheek. I throw my arms around her neck and I tell her all about my day. She listens patiently, and I can't help but have another tear when I tell her all I want is her. I need to pull myself together. I fetch her head collar and we walk side by side to the stable and have a therapeutic grooming session.

It's now 7.00pm and Mum suddenly appears leaning over the stable door watching us.

"So, this is the famous Bella, is it? She's absolutely beautiful Emily."

"Yes, this is Bella. Bella, meet Mum," I giggle.

Bella turns her head slowly and gently snorts at Mum. Holding her head collar, I slowly lead her across to meet Mum properly. Mum opens the stable door and Bella sniffs her. No bites, so she likes Mum. The three of us walk down to the field chatting as we go. I take off Bella's head collar, kiss her on her soft warm muzzle, and tell her once again how much I love her. She turns, canters off, then she suddenly stops in her tracks. She swings around to face us and lets out an almighty snort. Mum and I both laugh.

"What a character she is, she is so gorgeous Emily. I can see why you have fallen in love with her. She's a lot bigger in real life than in the photos you've shown me. Let's hope we hear from Janet soon. Mrs Evans gave me the name of the sanctuary Janet is helping at. They have one hundred and fifty-two dogs in their care. They really do an amazing job, so I've sent them a small donation to help," says Mum.

"That's so lovely of you Mum, you do so much for rescue dogs yourself. Maybe one day we could have a rescue sanctuary for ponies and dogs," I reply.

"Wouldn't that be a dream come true love, we need to win the lottery. But in the meantime, we can dream," laughs Mum.

We are now home; I have my dinner and give Mum and Dad a kiss goodnight. I'm so tired and desperately need my bed.

It seems ages before I eventually drop off to sleep, tossing this way and that, and once sleep claims me I dream of riding Bella. We're cantering through the woods, the sun is shining through the trees, and I'm laughing my head off one minute and singing at the top of my voice the next. Bella jumps a fallen tree and I shout, "Wow, Bella, that was truly spectacular," as I pat her gently on her neck.

I'm awake and sit bolt upright in bed. It was a dream, it isn't real at all is it? I return to reality with a bump and immediately feel sad and miserable. Why isn't Janet responding? I have googled the sanctuary in Thailand. They don't have regular Wi-Fi, and no-one knows where Janet is staying. I sigh again.

Sluggishly I drag myself out of bed, wash and dress then head off to do my usual paper round. Arriving back home I go into the kitchen where Mum is sitting deeply engrossed on her iPad. She turns her head towards me.

"Why aren't you smiling, Emily? It's your birthday tomorrow. Why don't you go to the riding school later? I'm sure Mrs Evans will be very grateful for your help and I know Bella will be pleased to see you."

"Ok Mum, I just wish we could get hold of Janet."

Opening my bedroom door, I slowly walk across to my window, stand and stare at the empty stable and paddocks letting out a long sigh.

I picture myself laughing with joy, running across the paddock with Bella chasing me. I turn away from the window as tears blur my vision. I change my clothes and go outside to get my bike.

I decide to stop on my way to the riding school to see Bill and Ben, knowing they always make me smile. "Bill, Ben," I call to them. They look up and come straight over to me. Bill puts his muzzle against my cheek, it's so soft and warm. I close my eyes and he blows air into my ear. It tickles, and I giggle for the first time today. Bill is probably feeling my emotions and is trying to make me feel better. He has certainly done that.

I feel much happier as I jump on my bike and cycle to the riding school.

My first stop is to trot down to see Bella, once again she lifts her head up and whinnies as she hears my voice. I truly love her with every ounce of my heart.

I work hard all morning at the riding school trying hard to blot out my disappointment. I ask Mrs Evans if she has any news but she still hasn't heard anything from Janet. I go up to my favourite place in the hay barn at lunchtime and shout across to Bella. She whinnies back to me but looks a bit concerned to see me so high up in the barn. I smile.

I really miss Kate now she's moved away with her family. I loved having her to talk things over with up here in the barn. We skype regularly but it isn't the same, I still wish she was here with me.

Before leaving the riding school late in the afternoon, I give Bella a huge hug and kiss.

"Bella, it's my birthday tomorrow. I will be fifteen years old and the best present in the whole wide world would be for us to be together for ever and ever." Tears roll down my face, and for the first time ever Bella licks my face and my tears away.

"Thank you Bella. I love you, and I promise I'll come and see you tomorrow."

Walking back up the path Mrs Evans appears and calls me over. She hands me an envelope. She smiles and wishes me a very happy birthday for tomorrow.

Soon I'm home; I have dinner, followed by a bath, wash my hair and decide to have an early night. I don't have to get up early for my paper round tomorrow as the friendly owner of the newsagents, Annette, has kindly given me the morning off as a birthday treat.

# Chapter 10

$*$ $*$ $*$

I AM SURE I CAN hear singing. I sit bolt upright in bed, rub my eyes and peer at my watch, I can just about make out it is eight o'clock. I'm confused as to what day of the week it is, and for a second I panic. My paper round! Then my brain kicks into gear and I remember, today is my birthday and I have the day off.

It's Mum and Dad singing 'Happy Birthday to you' outside my bedroom door. Tap tapping on the door before swinging it open, Mum and Dad walk in grinning at me.

"Come on birthday girl, get washed and dressed and we'll have a nice breakfast," urges Mum. I smile. I'm still tired and a bit down in the dumps, but I manage to drag myself out of bed.

We sit at the breakfast table in the kitchen, we have cereal, followed by jam on toast. Sighing, I glance up at the clock on the wall, it is 9.00am.

"Come on, let's all go for a nice walk. Some fresh air will do you good, and it will put some colour in your cheeks," suggests Dad. I sigh but nod.

Just as I am about to open the door to go outside, I hear a beep, beep noise in the distance.

Beep, beep, there it goes again. It's getting louder and louder and I can see Mrs Evans in her Land Rover pulling a trailer and coming up our drive. I am totally confused. I can't think straight. I'm sure I haven't arranged to go somewhere today with Mrs Evans. Or have I?

Mrs Evans turns the trailer around, and shouts to me through the window, "Happy birthday, Emily, dear. I was just on my way to the saddlery, and thought I'd drop off some spare hay and straw for you at the same time."

"Oh, thank you very much," I call back. "Would it be ok if we unload it at the back of the stable, where the other bales are?"

"No problem, dear," Mrs Evans shouts back.

I walk towards the stable as Mrs Evans reverses the trailer up to the yard. Mum and Dad are following close behind. *How lovely of them*, I think to myself. I can really do with some help to unload the bales. Dad must have read my mind as he smiles and says, "Can't leave the birthday girl to do all the hard work on her special day, now can we?"

Suddenly, I'm sure I can hear a whinny coming from the trailer. Silly me. Now I can hear another whinny, and this time it's much louder.

Mum and Dad are right behind me, and Dad puts his hands on my shoulders. I'm so confused and feel as if my feet are glued to the ground.

The ramp of the trailer slowly lowers.

"Happy birthday, darling," Mum and Dad whisper together. I really don't understand what's going on. We just need to get the hay and straw unloaded don't we? The ramp is halfway down now and for a second I'm sure I see something move. I can't breathe. The ramp is all the way down now, and I just stand and look with my mouth wide open.

No, oh no, no, it can't be... "Oh, yes, yes, yes, yes!" I scream. Standing right in front of me is my Bella. My legs have gone to jelly. I feel weak and wobbly, and I'm shaking. I can't move.

"Go on love," says Dad, gently. "Go and bring your Bella, into her new home."

I don't need telling twice and slowly walk up the ramp urging my legs to start working properly. My birthday dream has come true. Very quickly my legs come back to life and I race up the ramp, and throw my arms around Bella's neck. Tears are streaming down my face. "Oh, thank you, oh, thank you, oh, thank you" I somehow manage between gasping for breath. I give her a massive kiss, look at her and I cannot believe my eyes, my Bella has a single tear running down her cheek. I gently wipe it away and hug her tight.

At last Bella and I are together! What is meant to be, is meant to be.

# Chapter 11

* * *

MY TEARS HAVE SLOWLY STOPPED flowing and I can just about see again as I slowly lead Bella down the ramp. How beautiful she looks. Bella stops at halfway to have a look around, I gently stroke her neck. She's so warm and soft to touch. At some stage, without me even knowing, Uncle Gary must have arrived. Turning to look at him, I grin and I am one hundred per cent positive he's wiping his eyes with a tissue! I will tease him another time.

I feel as if I'm in a dream world, I need someone to pinch me so I know this is actually real.

As I walk Bella to her stable, Mrs Evans walks beside me and explains what had happened.

"Janet called me yesterday afternoon, dear. She hadn't been able to receive any messages due to having no signal. She had a day off from the sanctuary and went to visit a friend when she suddenly started to receive numerous texts from me. To cut a long story short, dear, she really didn't want to sell Ballerina but I explained about the bond you have built up with Bella over the last two years. I emailed her photographs of the two of you and when she saw how happy the two of you are together she couldn't resist and finally agreed. There is one condition though".

I hold my breath.

"If at any time in the future you don't want Bella anymore, you need to sign an agreement which states she will be returned back to me at the riding school and Janet will continue to pay for her keep. I knew you would agree to this, Emily, and that's what I told Janet."

I let out a deep breath, and for the first time in two years I really want to hug Mrs Evans. I can't stop myself and wrap my arms tightly around her as I thank her for all her help. I eventually let go, look at her and I'm sure I can see a tear in her eye.

"You're welcome, dear," she replies, as she pulls a tissue from her sleeve to wipe her eye.

"Oh, Mrs Evans, you've been so amazing. How much has Janet agreed to sell Bella to me for?"

"£100.00, dear."

I gasp. "£100.00? That's peanuts. Are you sure that's what she said?"

"Very sure, dear. Janet said the right home is more important than money, and the £100.00 you will pay her, she's donating straight to the dog sanctuary. She really is an amazing lady, Emily, with a huge heart."

I'm speechless. I've saved £900. I only have to pay £100.

"Mrs Evans, I'm still in shock. I will pay her £100.00, but I will also make a separate donation of £100.00 to the sanctuary she is helping in Thailand. Would this be ok?"

"Emily, Janet will be thrilled. You remind me of her when she was younger. You have a very big heart, and you are a natural around animals."

I grin and have a lump in my throat at the same time.

"I'd better get a bed ready for Bella, right now," I fuss.

Mum comes to my side laughing, "No need to worry. After you had gone to bed last night, Jodie came over and helped me and your Dad get the stable ready. To be honest, we all enjoyed it, we do hope it's up to your very high standards."

Leading Bella into her new stable, I remove her head collar and lead rope and pass them to Mrs. Evans who hangs them up on a nearby hook. Bella immediately gets down into her lovely straw bed and has a good old roll around. Roll to the left, roll to the right, very comical and a wonderful sight, one I certainly didn't expect to be seeing today. I can't help but laugh as she gets up, she has straw everywhere. She looks straight at me, snorts, shakes herself and looks very pleased with herself.

I can hear Mum asking Uncle Gary and Mrs Evans if they would like to go into the house for tea or coffee to leave me to spend some time with Bella.

At last we're alone. Time for me to explain once again to Bella how hard I've been saving for years, doing household chores, getting up early every morning to do my paper round in sunshine, in rain, in wind, and in snow. Bella is patiently listening and is looking at me with a comical expression as I begin to tell her a funny story.

"Bella, it was a freezing cold morning. The snow was very deep. I carefully walked up a garden path to deliver their newspaper when suddenly I heard a voice say, 'Morning.' I turned around and to my sheer amazement standing there was a snowman. I walked towards the snowman and was actually thinking to myself, *Emily don't be so silly, snowmen can't talk.* There was no-one else to be seen. I was just about to turn around and walk on when a child jumped out from behind the snowman and loudly shouted 'Boo.' At this precise moment I screamed, slipped over and as I jumped backwards in fright, I ended up flat on my back with my poor newspaper bag flying up in the air. The next moment, the child's father came running out of their house. He had heard my scream, and seeing me sprawled on the ground could not apologize enough for his son's behaviour, as he helped me up off the ground. Slowly brushing all the snow off myself, I was so thankful I wasn't hurt. In fact, I had to giggle to myself afterwards, once I eventually saw the funny side of it."

An hour later, after continuously chatting to Bella, I decide it's time to leave her to have a proper rest but before I leave, I mention to Bella that I've hundreds of stories to tell her. I'm sure Bella let out a big sigh, but it could have been my imagination. I fetch a little more hay to put in her hay rack, and gallop back to the bungalow shouting to her "Be a good girl, see you in a little while."

I am on cloud nine as I walk through the kitchen door.

Aunty Lynette has arrived and she jumps up to give me a birthday hug. I put my arms around her and thank her for coming. It's now time to open all my birthday cards.

My biggest surprise is in the envelope Mrs Evans gave me yesterday as I left the yard. It contains a fax with confirmation of insurance for one year with cover for Bella for up to £3,500 veterinary cover. Also, a note inside the card reads:

*Dear Emily,*
*Happy 15th birthday! Everyone here at the riding school has had a whip round and enclosed is Bella's insurance policy for one year. Thank you for all your help over the last two years. We will miss you helping out, but hope you and Bella will visit us regularly.*
*Lots of love, Mrs Evans, Jodie, all the girls and lads and of course not forgetting lots of love from all the ponies' and Jack and Jill xxx*

I have a lump in my throat and tears are threatening again!

Dad hands me Bella's veterinary certificate which I eagerly look at. I'm so happy. Bella has recently had her yearly flu and tetanus jab. She has also recently been wormed, this is great news to me financially. Mum explains to me she now has Janet's bank details and if I give her £100.00 she will bacs it across to her for Bella. Mum and Dad love my idea of sending the £100.00 donation to the dog sanctuary and Mum says she will bacs this for me too.

I will still have £700.00 left over after paying for Bella and I've also received money in my birthday cards from friends and family members.

My new total after paying for Bella amounts to £925.00. Wow, I am financially stable, this is totally awesome, Bella will want for nothing.

Another lovely and very generous gift from our family members, uncles, aunts and each set of grandparents is that they have generously donated £35.00 each to the local dog sanctuary where Mum works tirelessly every spare moment she has. Mum is thrilled because they need all the help they can get. I'm going to give Mum £50.00 in £1 coins for her sanctuary also. This will still leave me with £875.00.

It is now lunchtime and Uncle Gary and Aunty Lynette say their goodbyes and head home. Mrs. Evans had to leave earlier as she had lessons to teach. I announce that I'm going to check on Bella and Mum decides to come too.

As we approach the stable, Bella whinnies and makes my heart jump. She's already drunk over half of her water and seems very content. I gently put on her new head collar with lead rope attached and slowly lead her out to the paddock, closely followed by Mum.

Bella eagerly looks around and for a second she stands very tall, and her nostrils expand. She releases a very large snort that makes Mum jump. I can't help but giggle.

"Wow," says Mum "She's so beautiful."

I take off her head collar and Bella puts her head high into the air and trots off. She prances and snorts as she checks out her new home. *'What a lovely mover you are Bella',* I think to myself but once again I have said it out loud. Mum giggles again.

After a few minutes, she settles down and is munching the lovely green grass contentedly. Occasionally she looks up, glances around and then settles back down to graze. I walk across to check her water bucket in the field and see that it's full.

"Mum, can I get a towel out of the airing cupboard? I want to lie on the grass and watch Bella?"

"Of course love, come with me and I'll find you one."

Back indoors, Mum rummages around in the airing cupboard and generously hands me a big bath towel. "Here you are love, this should be big enough for you. You can keep it for the yard, we have plenty of towels."

I gallop back to the paddock and Bella sees me coming and walks towards me. I swear she is smiling at me.

Spreading the towel out onto the grass, very near to where Bella is standing, I sit down and roll onto my side, prop my head up on my hand and my whole body feels full of love for my beautiful Bella. I still can't believe it's real and my dream has at last come true.

I chat away to Bella, I am sure she has realised over the last two years what a chatterbox I am. "Bella, you and I are going to have lots of fun. We'll ride for miles and I'll spend hours grooming and loving you, and guess what? I am now officially your mummy!" I giggle out aloud.

I glance at my watch, it is 5.00pm and time for me to get everything ready for Bella's bedtime. I remove the droppings from her stable, fluff up the lovely deep straw bed, make up a small feed, top up her water and bring her back in. She walks nicely by my side to her stable and waits patiently whilst I fetch her food.

Bella is busy eating, so I go and get some more hay. I'm not going to groom her today, she has had such a long day and needs to settle. She has licked her feed bucket clean but I wash it anyway and make up a small feed for the morning. I must go to the saddlery tomorrow to get some fly spray. There have been a few around today, they really are a nuisance.

Mum and Dad arrive at the stable door to tell me dinner is ready. I check everything is tidy, make sure the stable bolt and kick latch are on, the tack room is padlocked and the yard gate properly shut. I blow Bella a kiss, and tell her it's now time for my dinner. "Love you Bella," I call as I gallop to catch up Mum and Dad. I have no problem eating my dinner tonight. I'm so hungry and enjoy every scrap, just like Bella.

# Chapter 12

* * *

I LOOK AT MY WATCH and see it is now 10.00pm, nearly my bedtime. I need to go out and check on Bella. I let myself quietly out of the back door, and walk quickly to the yard. Smiling as the floodlight comes on, I walk as silently as I can across to the stable, lean over the bottom part of the door, and switch on the push-on light. My heart once again is instantly filled with love.

Bella is lying down in her golden straw bed, fast asleep. Either she senses me or the light being switched on, because first she opens one eye, then the other and blinks a few times as she adjusts to the light. Lifting her head off the straw, she sees me looking in at her and gives me a delightful little whinny. My heart jumps and I quietly open the stable door, walk in and close the door behind me before walking across to her. Kneeling down by her side I gently and slowly stroke her soft beautiful neck. She hasn't moved and lets out a huge sigh of contentment as I gently kiss her on her muzzle.

She is warm and relaxed as I continue to stroke her, talking to her in a quiet voice, almost a whisper. All of a sudden, an overwhelming feeling of tiredness engulfs me, I snuggle down next to Bella and lay my head on her neck. I am so cosy and comfortable; my eyelids start to feel very heavy and before long I'm fast asleep.

✳  ✳  ✳

Slowly waking up, I notice it is daylight and I'm in my own bed? Did I dream I was cuddling Bella in her stable last night?

At this precise moment Mum pops her head around my bedroom door. As she opens my curtains she explains to me that she and Dad had come to say goodnight at about 11.00pm. Finding I wasn't in my bedroom they had guessed I'd sneaked out to see Bella, and had found me fast asleep with my head resting on Bella's neck.

Mum continues, "I crept back to the bungalow to fetch the camera and I took a beautiful photograph of the two of you snuggled up. Your Dad carefully lifted you into his arms, I had to laugh as he moaned and groaned about you not being little anymore and it wasn't helping his back, as he struggled to carry you to bed."

This made me smile.

'Emily, you didn't even open your eyes. Your birthday excitement must have totally worn you out."

"I guess so," I manage.

# Chapter 13

*  *  *

I QUICKLY GLANCE AT MY watch; it is 6.30am. I spring out of bed, and run across to look out of my window. I can see Bella's head over the stable door. I wave and just stop myself calling out to her, remembering that Dad is still in bed. I dress as fast as I can, and rush out to see my Bella. As I get nearer to the stable, I can't resist, "Bella, Bella," I call. She turns her head in my direction and lets out a little whinny. My heart is jumping for joy.

I open the stable door, and give Bella a big cuddle before getting her breakfast. After she's finished eating I pick out her hooves before turning her out into the paddock for a good old roll and run around. I hurry back to the stable, muck out and leave her bedding piled up around the sides, so the floor can dry once I've swept it clean. Washing out Bella's feed and water buckets, I now make up her afternoon feed.

I gallop back to the bungalow at full speed, I wash myself, gobble down some toast and head off to do my paper round, still wearing my jodhpurs. I'm so happy and sing all the way as I push the papers quickly through the letterboxes.

Back home, and carelessly dropping my bike, I run across to check on Bella and I'm relieved to see she's still happily grazing. Phew!

Making sure she has enough water to drink, I give her a big kiss and head off to find Mum.

After a slice of toast and something to drink, Mum and I hang out the washing and we head off to the local saddlery.

With the voucher I received for my birthday from Aunty Sharon, I want to buy a lovely cob size leather bridle in dark brown, with a loose ring snaffle bit. The man in the saddlery is very helpful as usual, and I tell him I also want a saddle. We agree that he will come out see us the day after tomorrow to try a few on Bella, so we can select one that fits her properly. After purchasing a bottle of herbal fly spray, our next stop is the bank to change all my coins into notes.

I chat away to the lady in the bank. I explain to her all about my new pony Bella. She actually has a tear in her eye as I tell her about Bella's poor start, how I fell in love with her the first time I saw her and desperately wanted to buy her for my birthday. It didn't look like it was going to happen at all, but then she was delivered on the morning of my birthday and what an awesome surprise it all was. I am talking ten to the dozen. I didn't realise there was a queue in the bank until I suddenly hear what seems to be a muffled cry. I glance around to see six people, three of them ladies, are all wiping their eyes. They smile at me as I make my way to the door and I grin back at them.

Back home, we only have time for a quick snack, as Dad appears in the doorway and asks, "Shall we all take Bella out for a walk around the village, as it's such a lovely day?"

"What a great idea, thanks Dad," I eagerly reply.

We all head outside and I fetch Bella in from the paddock, bring her to the yard, and give her a quick groom, check her feet to make sure she doesn't have any stones in them, and put on her new bridle.

I adjust a few straps here and there, to make sure it fits perfectly. I stand back and stare at her. She looks so pretty. I attach two lead ropes onto the bit and while I walk on the near side, Dad has a lead rope and walks on the other side, with Mum taking the lead, walking out in front.

We decide it's safer for all of us to go out together to start with, until we know how Bella behaves on the roads.

The four of us walk down a long twisting lane with a mixture of beech trees, oak trees, chestnut trees and fir trees lining each side, and the sun is shining through gaps in the leaves. A car is slowly coming towards us. I hold my arm out to the side, move it slowly up and down asking the driver to slow down; then holding my arm out straight in front of me with my fingers pointing to the sky for the car to stop. I feel a bit like a lollypop lady but the driver of the car kindly obliges. Bella walks past the car perfectly, and smiling I thank the driver and tell Bella what a good girl she is.

In the distance, we can hear a loud noise. "Sounds like a tractor to me, just be on your guard," warns Mum, turning around to face us.

A few minutes later and sure enough a tractor slowly comes around the bend up ahead. Seeing us, the driver pulls over to the side and stops to let us pass by. Bella doesn't even flinch and we express our thanks as we walk on. I'm so proud of Bella, and pat her on her neck gently saying, "Well done, you are such a good girl!" as we continue on our walk. It's such a relief to see for ourselves that Bella is good in traffic. This means Mum and Dad won't worry too much when I'm out riding on my own.

We've been out for almost an hour and a half and have thoroughly enjoyed ourselves and Bella is happy and relaxed too. We've met some neighbours walking their dogs, seen a rabbit, various ponies in fields and Bella has enjoyed a few polo mints along the way. Actually, we probably haven't walked all that far, as we've spent a lot of the time stopping and chatting to people along the way. It's a good job Bella is so patient and laid back now.

There is only one slight hiccup when Bella decides she wants to walk up a neighbours' drive to investigate what is at the other end, and have a look in a window or two. Dad and I are taken unaware, but manage to turn her quite quickly before she has gone too far. Unfortunately though, on the way back down the path, Bella grabs a rather large yellow flower in her mouth. This is still attached to a beautiful bush and Bella is pulling hard on the flower to detach it. Luckily the bush is on my side of the path so I am able to grab it and pull it away from her before she can pull the whole thing out of the ground. I don't think Bella likes the taste very much. I glance back at the house calling my apologies to the lady looking out of the window as Bella is busy spitting out bits of the flower all over the path. Luckily I can see the lady laughing. Phew.

Mum is waiting patiently at the bottom of the path for us. She has her hand to her mouth, her shoulders are shaking and she has a twinkle in her eye. She manages to blurt out, "Well that's one thing you forgot to tell us Emily, how nosey and cheeky Bella is!"

✳ ✳ ✳

The following morning we all take Bella out for another walk; this time we take a different route and Bella is perfectly behaved and thankfully leaves the neighbours flowers alone.

This afternoon the man from the saddlery is due and bringing with him various saddles. Hopefully he'll have one that will fit Bella.

He arrives promptly in his big van, and as he opens the door I can see several saddles in the back, all different in one way or another.

One saddle after another is placed on Bella's back. She is very patient and looks to be enjoying all the attention. Eventually we find one that is the perfect fit, a lovely synthetic saddle and it is very comfy for both of us.

Over the next few days we continue to take Bella out for long walks and we are now confident she is 100% safe in traffic. I continue to spend as much time as I can with her, and sit in the paddock drawing pictures as she quietly grazes. More sketches to go on my bedroom wall!

I sing to her, I chat to her, Bella adores it when I run my hands up and down her neck hugging her as I tell her how much I love her.

# Chapter 14

* * *

A WEEK HAS FLOWN BY since my birthday. A whole week that Bella has been mine. I still have to pinch myself to make sure it's all real.

Today Mrs Evans and Jodie arrive to watch me ride Bella for the first time in her new home. Tacking her up, Mrs Evans admires her new saddle and bridle. She double checks both all over making sure she is happy with everything. She remarks on the lovely

plait I have put in her forelock. I lead Bella out to the spare paddock, Jodie holds Bella, whilst I get on board.

Mrs Evans calls out, "What a picture you both look dear."

I still find it hard to believe that at last, after years of dreaming, I'm sitting on my *dream pony* at home, and Bella feels perfect. Mum and Dad appear at the side of the paddock, and Mum is clicking away taking photos. Dad is smiling, I'm smiling, in fact everyone is smiling, and I'm sure Bella is too.

Once on board Mrs Evans asks me to check the girth. I lean down and dutifully do this and she asks me to walk Bella in a large circle, then to trot her, and then bring her back to a walk. Perfect.

After 10 minutes of repeating this, Bella is warming up nicely and I ask her to go into a canter by gently pressing my heels into her stomach. Bella obliges and in her excitement, manages to put in a hefty buck! I can hear Mum's quick intake of breath, and Dad can't disguise an 'Oh!' but when we realise that's it, we all relax and everyone laughs. At least I stay on.

Before she leaves, Mrs Evans advises me to ride Bella in the paddock regularly, until we feel one hundred per cent confident about venturing out onto the roads alone. She informs me I can then ride Bella over to the riding school and take her into the indoor school, where she will help me teach Bella to jump.

During the following week, Bella and I have lots of fun together riding in the paddock. Bella enjoys putting in a little buck whenever she gets excited but this doesn't worry me, in fact it makes me laugh.

For a bit of fun I have even ridden Bella bareback, (Mrs Evans probably wouldn't have approved, and I'm sure neither would my parents!) but I enjoy it as Bella is so comfy to sit on.

Today I am grooming Bella in the stable, she is loving it, so much so she is nodding off. I stand back and admire her shiny coat and I have a sudden urge to see if I could jump on board. Bella turns to look at me as if she knows I am up to something. After numerous attempts, I manage it, but then slide off the other side head first into the straw. Bella is patiently putting up with my behaviour and turns her head to look down at me in disgust as I sit on the floor. She actually looks as if she is frowning and tutting at me. I laugh out loud and Bella snorts.

Most of my family have popped over at some point during the last week to see me riding Bella. When Chris came over to see us, he came armed with his riding hat, and begged me to let him ride her. "Ok," I'd agreed. He really enjoyed himself, walking and trotting her around the paddock and on dismounting he turned to me and said, "I think I've fallen in love with your pony."

"No chance, hands off, she's mine!" I had replied laughing.

Today I decide to telephone Mrs Evans to see if we can go over to the riding school this afternoon. She happily agrees.

Two o'clock, Bella and I are on our way, closely followed by Mum riding her bike, as she insists on coming too.

Bella is perfectly behaved on the way over and when we arrive, everyone comes rushing over to admire her. She's thoroughly enjoying all the attention and fuss she's getting. With several hands stroking her, patting her and telling her how gorgeous she is, I just sit on board beaming proudly. Nobody could have done this two years ago. It's a real shame that Kate has moved, I do miss her. I've emailed her lots of photographs of Bella, and she has messaged back saying she has now fallen in love with Bella too and she cannot believe she is the same pony. We continue to email each other at least twice a week and occasionally skype.

Mrs Evans suddenly appears in the yard. "Good afternoon Bella, and Emily dear. Please ride over to the school. I've put some jumping poles out ready for you. Wait a minute though, dear, can you just ride over to see Jodie. I think we should put some brushing boots on Bella to protect her front legs in case she knocks the poles."

We find Jodie, who quickly locates a pair that fit Bella, and informs me we can use them whenever we want. I thank her and we make our way to the school.

I warm Bella up and after ten minutes Mrs Evans asks me to walk her over the poles. Bella looks at these with great interest and gingerly walks over them, but then turns her head and snorts at them in disgust.

We repeat this over and over again until Bella seems happier. Now it's time to try trotting over the poles but Bella has different ideas. She isn't trotting over them at all, she's taking flying leaps trying to jump them all in one go. She's obviously finding this great fun, but I'm struggling, she is so strong. I am trying my hardest to keep her under some sort of control and grab hold of as much of her mane as I can, but in mid-flight, I lose my reins - where they go remains a mystery to me - my legs fly out at the sides, I lose my stirrups and the saddle seems a couple of feet away from my rump. All this appears to be happening in slow motion but what goes up must come down, and I do just that. Bella lands beautifully but I crash back down into the saddle.

"OUCH".

Leaning forward and desperately trying to stay on, my arms are now wrapped around Bella's neck. Before I know it, I've landed face down in a heap on the school floor. I'm so embarrassed, and to be honest a little winded.

Mrs Evans comes rushing over to help me to my feet and to make sure no bones are broken. She also helps to brush off some of the sand from my clothes. My mouth seems to be full of sand, so I wipe it on my sleeve. Patting me on my shoulder she says jovially, "Never mind dear, you're not a proper rider until you've had a few falls."

"WHAT!"

Once Bella realises I am not on board any longer, she at least stops and waits for me. She is standing patiently waiting only a few feet away watching me with a very comical expression, which I interpret as, *that was fun, can we do it again? Next time Mum, please try and stay on my back!*

I can see Mum out of the corner of my eye. She's standing ridged with her white knuckles jammed into her mouth, but she relaxes when she sees I'm ok. I hope she didn't have her camera ready for that one! Mrs Evans helps me back into the saddle.

"Now Emily, this time I suggest you keep Bella on a very tight rein," says Mrs Evans. "You'll find you have more control."

I nod and we try again, this really does work. Bella is now trotting proudly and beautifully over the poles and she doesn't attempt to leap into the air. We've done this five times now, and Mrs Evans agrees she is satisfied as the fifth attempt was "perfect!" Now it's time for a small cavaletti jump. I'm sure Bella is thinking, *this is more like it,* because she clears the jump by at least three feet!

Bella is getting very excited and in her excitement gives a huge buck. I laugh as I pull her back into a walk. Her neck is damp and foamy from all the hard work, and I can feel my hair sticking to my scalp under my riding hat.

My arms are beginning to ache too, as well as other parts of my body. Mrs Evans now thinks that we've done enough for today and asks me to dismount. I do so but my legs have gone weak and give way as I hit the ground and I go plop again onto the school floor. But I'm on a high, I get up and notice Mrs Evans is smiling again. I've never seen her smile so much in such a short space of time. Her voice brings me out of my daydream. 'I'll hold Bella for you Emily dear. Will you go and ask Jodie to lend you a cavesson head collar, I'm sure Bella would love a really good roll and probably a run around after all her hard work.' As I leave the school, she adds, 'Please also ask Jodie to put the kettle on. I'm truly parched, and also rinse your mouth out well dear, otherwise you'll be crunching on sand for the rest of the day.'

I am not too sure what 'parched' means, I've never heard this word before but decide not to stop and ask her in case I make myself look stupid, *I'll google it later!* I didn't think she'd seen me get a mouthful of sand when I fell off. She doesn't miss a thing that Mrs Evans.

A few minutes later, I'm back in the school with the cavesson head collar and thank Mrs Evans very much for all the help she has

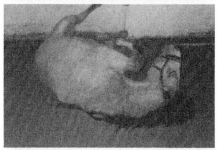

given me today. There's that smile again. She helps me untack Bella and I put the head collar on her and give her a big kiss.

Within seconds of me letting go of Bella, she trots off and gets down in the dark sand to have a good roll. She rolls to the left, then to the right and is now on her back with her legs up in the air. Getting up, she paws the sand again, goes back down and repeats it all over again! She lays still for a moment looking very content, up she gets, has a good shake and blinks her eyes a few times letting out a very big sigh. We all chuckle, and I am so glad Mum has her camera out this time. These are going to be fantastic photographs, and I can't wait to download them later.

I make my way over to Bella and gently wipe the sand from her eyes. She's covered in sand and where she has sweated so much, the sand has literally stuck all the way up her neck! It looks as if Bella has suddenly changed colour again with the dark sand all over her. Mrs Evans trots off to get a soft body brush and I groom Bella until all the sand has gone.

Bella has obviously enjoyed her first jumping adventure in the riding school! I give her a big hug, tack her up again and feel I am on 'cloud nine' as we ride home chatting to Mum who is at my side on her bike.

Every Saturday over the following three months I continue to take Bella along to the riding school and with the help of Mrs Evans, I think we've come a long way.

I did fall off again when Bella jumped a three-foot fence and she decided to put in a big buck at the same time which I wasn't prepared for. I landed flat out in the sand but thankfully wasn't hurt thanks to the soft landing.

Bella did walk over to me this time as if she was saying *'what are you doing on the floor again'*! I laughed at her expression, brushed myself down and got straight back on.

I've also been able to ride in the paddock after school but it's now dark by 4.30pm, and it is impossible for me to ride out on the roads.

Once a week I give Bella a lunge in the field. This is something different for her and we both enjoy it. The very first time I tried to lunge her was hilarious. I walked over to the paddock holding the lunge whip. Bella eyeballed it and backed away snorting. I laid it on the grass for her to have a closer look she then pounced on it with both front hooves, backed off and jumped on it again, snorting. I think she thought it was a snake as the string at the end is about 6 foot long and as I move it around, it wriggles! Bella soon got used to what we now call the 'snake'.

On Sundays the two of us go for nice long rides on the Downs. This is the highlight of my week. The Downs are just so beautiful. I love the way the trees change colour through the seasons. I've met so many new people, horse riders and lots of dog walkers too, and we often stop for a chat.

Bella seems to love dogs. She always puts her head down low, curiously smelling and looks at them as if she's having a conversation with them. The dogs we've met have always been very friendly and Uncle Gary has also been over quite a few times with Bailey and Millie. Bella did try and chase Millie out of her field and Millie just stood there barking at her, totally refusing to stop until Bella came over for Millie to lick her muzzle. How sweet.

# Chapter 15

* * *

COUNTING DOWN THE HOURS AT school has become a daily habit as I just want to rush home to see my Bella.

Sometimes the days really seem to drag. Looking up at the clock on the old brick wall, I swear the hands are going backwards not forwards.

Thankfully Mum now works from home and pops out now and again to check on Bella for me. This is such a relief and really does put my mind at rest.

We're now into December and only three weeks to go until Christmas Day. I've been very busy getting Bella's Christmas stocking ready. She's going to be so spoilt. So far she has herbal treats, a salt lick, a mineral stick, a saddle bag which will come in handy when we go out on long rides and a new fluffy red numnah to go under her saddle to keep her cosy throughout the winter months.

Finally, it is the last day of school. I rush home faster than the wind to tell Bella I have no more school for two weeks! I still have homework to complete but have plenty of time to get this done. *'Whoop, whoop,'* I cry out to her. By now Bella is used to my weird behaviour and my funny old sayings, and always gives me a gentle whinny whenever I approach. I'm sure she chuckles to herself although I can't be sure of that.

It's Christmas Eve and I'm outside in the cold night air hanging Bella's Christmas stocking onto her stable door. She stares at me with a very confused but comical expression. I'm singing Christmas songs and in between rambling, I inform her, "Bella, you will have to go to sleep quickly tonight because a man with a long white beard and dressed in a red suit, will be flying around the world on a sleigh pulled by reindeers. His name is Father Christmas and he'll be delivering presents to everyone, including you. Bella, my motto is you are never too old to believe in Father Christmas". Do ponies raise eyebrows? I am sure Bella can. I think if she could talk, she'd be saying, *'Now this time you have really lost the plot!'* But bless her heart, she carries on listening, well I like to think she is.

Now it is time for me to gallop back to the bungalow to have a nice long soak in the bath as I am feeling exhausted. Dressed in my PJ's and feeling refreshed I trot outside to say goodnight to Bella and check that she has everything she needs. Happy all is well, I leave her in peace and return to the bungalow, canter to my bedroom, fly through the door and fall flat on my face onto my bed. I have no energy left. I manage to more or less crawl to the bathroom, then shortly after, back to the bedroom, switch off the light and plop into bed. Bliss!

5.30am and I'm wide awake. It's still very dark outside and I lean over to switch on my bedside lamp. I lie still, feeling a little weary. It suddenly dawns on me that today is Christmas Day. "Wicked," I accidentally shout out loud!

Jumping out of bed, I trip over my slippers and just about manage to stop myself landing in a heap on the floor, I get a fit of the giggles and pull myself together as Mum and Dad are still asleep. Grabbing my dressing gown and stifling my giggles, I run to the bathroom to get washed. Back to the bedroom, dress quickly and now I am galloping up the hallway to the lounge to see if I have any presents under the tree and as I open the door I can see a pile of presents sitting under the tree. *'Can they be mine? Oh, I do hope so'.*

Mum and Dad eventually appear in the lounge, although Dad looks tired and is rubbing his eyes grumbling about it being too early. We all wish each other a Merry Christmas, Mum rushes out to put the kettle on and I begin opening my presents. I'm thrilled as my main present is a much-needed pay as you go mobile phone from Mum and Dad. Their one stipulation is that I carry this with me at all times, especially when out riding on my own. It will make them feel happier if I can quickly make contact if there is ever an emergency.

I have already received the saddle for Bella back in August, as part of an early Christmas present from Mum and Dad and the money I receive from family and friends goes straight to them as promised.

Having finished opening my presents and hugging and thanking Mum and Dad, it's now time to rush out to help Bella open hers and so leaving Mum and Dad to enjoy an early cup of tea, I bolt out of the back door.

'Merry Christmas Bella,' I call as I run towards the stable. 'Come on Bella, let's see what Father Christmas has left for you shall we?'

Bella is still lying down in her fresh straw bed but opens one eye and stares at me. I'm sure she is thinking, '*Oh no, she's still talking about the man in the red suit flying around the sky at night. Also, what time in the morning do you call this?*'

'Come on Bella, up you get,' I coax. Obligingly if a little slowly, she gets to her feet, stretches her neck and sticks one of her back legs straight out behind her.

'Goodness, I didn't know you could do that!'

Bella opens her mouth and produces an enormous yawn showing an amazing number of large teeth before slowly walking to the stable door.

I hold out one of Bella's presents which I have just taken out of her Christmas stocking for her to see. She must know what is inside as she quickly rips the paper off the herbal treats. She looks very impressed and curls her top lip up at me. I open the treat bag wide and hand her another one, she makes short work of this and I let her have a third one, this too is gone in a flash! She's probably now thinking, '*I quite like the man in the red suit Mum calls Father Christmas. I do hope he comes regularly*'. I take her treats away and I'm sure she's now thinking, '*Charming, how rude. The man in the red suit left them for me, you have only given me three treats? How mean is that when there's a whole bag full*'.

I show her the red numnah, it's so fluffy and soft. I explain this will keep her warm and the saddle bag is for when we go out together on long rides. She doesn't seem at all interested.

It's now time for Bella to open her Christmas card handmade lovingly by me. On the front is a photo of the two of us. I show it to her and she licks it curling her lip up again. I ignore her behaviour, I look at the photo which now has bits of herbal treat sticking to it, and continue to read the words out to her. 'Merry Christmas to my Bella, I love you with all my heart, Mummy, kiss, kiss, kiss.' I grin as Bella puts her herbal muzzle on my cheek. This must be her way of saying thank you but before I can stop her she leans forward and grabs the card. This results in a bit of a tussle before she lets go, the card now has a good set of teeth marks right across the top. I can't feel annoyed with her though and she did give me a kiss on the cheek beforehand. I pin the card right at the top of the stable door so Bella can't reach it, and gaze up at it. Even though it is a little battered it now looks more personal.

This may seem rather silly but I have also made myself a card from Bella. I thank her and pin this next to the other card. I smile again and gallop back to the bungalow for an early breakfast.

I have a couple of surprises for Mum and Dad too. Dad and I have arranged a special surprise for Mum, but she can't have this until mid-morning. How I'm going to keep this secret today of all days is going to be very hard.

Mum and Dad are sitting at the kitchen table having another cup of tea and hot buttered toast which smells really good. I rush to my bedroom, gallop back and sit down at the kitchen table. From behind my back I put four brightly wrapped Christmas presents on the table, two for each of them. The look of surprise on their faces is just magic.

"Open them up then," I urge, and they both eagerly tear off the wrapping paper from their respective gifts at exactly the same time. For Dad, I've bought him some of his favourite humbugs and a new wallet. For Mum, a warm, soft scarf for the cold days outside, and some of her special chocolates. They both seem thrilled.

"Well it can't be just me and Bella who receive presents on Christmas day can it?" I laugh. We sit and chat for a while and twenty minutes later Mum and Dad dash off to get washed and changed.

I gallop back out to the stable, feed Bella and once she's finished I turn her out into her paddock whilst I muck out. I finish off and make sure Bella has everything she needs and return to the kitchen to help Mum prepare the vegetables ready for our Christmas meal.

Dad is popping out to wish a close neighbour Merry Christmas, and to collect Mum's surprise present. He'll be back in about an hour. Mum, and I enjoy each other's company whilst we potter about the kitchen and listen to Christmas songs on the radio.

Just over an hour later Dad pops his head around the kitchen door to let us know he's back. He gives me a wink and a nod when Mum isn't looking.

"Is everything alright Dad?" I ask him.

"Everything's just fine love. Would you please come and help me with something?" Dad replies. I can hear the excitement in his voice. I am now feeling very excited too as I follow him outside to the car. He stands aside so I can open the estate boot. Leaning in and using both of his hands Dad scoops up the special gift as quickly as he can and heads back to the lounge, leaving me to close and lock the car.

The lounge door is shut when I get back indoors, but hearing me come in, Dad opens it slightly and gives me the thumbs up.

"Emily, please could you ask your Mum to come in here for a moment?" whispers Dad.

"Mum, Dad says he wants you in the lounge," I tell her, trying to sound casual. "Ok love, but I'll have to be back in a minute or two to put the potatoes on."

At last she is leaving the kitchen and heading for the lounge, I quietly tiptoe behind her and can actually hear my heart pounding.

"Why have you shut the lounge door?" asks Mum opening it. She walks in, I hear her gasp, then she squeals and an excited bark comes from the other side of the lounge. "Suki, oh my Suki," whispers Mum, as she rushes across the room and engulfs the medium size dog in her arms. Tears are pouring down her face, and Suki is trying to lick them away, her tail is wagging like mad.

"Merry Christmas love," Dad whispers to Mum. "You mean she's mine to keep?" "Yes, she's all yours, forever. We know how much you've been missing her now you are working from home, and she's been missing you too. So I arranged with the dog rescue people, (Dad can never remember names of organisations), that Suki must come to live with us." Mum is speechless and just gulps and hugs Suki even more.

In the past Suki had been found wandering the streets, starving and in very poor condition. She could only have been about fourteen months old at the time, still a baby really. Mum was volunteering at the rescue centre and spent hours and hours looking after and caring for Suki and they had built up a very special bond. Suki had been pining and missing Mum dreadfully since she'd decided to work from home and we know Mum has definitely been missing her even though she's never let on to me or Dad. Recently Dad overheard Mum on the telephone to her friend saying how much she is missing Suki and this is when Dad came up with his plan to reunite the two of them.

"Oh, she looks so smart with her red bow around her neck," coos Mum. "Would you like a drink my Suki? Oh no, we don't have bowls for her and the pet shops are most probably shut today", says Mum with panic in her voice. "I think there are still some Christmas presents behind the tree, have a look," suggests Dad.

Standing up from where she has been down on her knees hugging Suki, Mum walks to the back of the tree and emerges with an armful of presents. "Who are these for?" she says to Suki sitting back down onto the floor. "Would you like to help unwrap your presents Suki?" Suki doesn't need asking twice, and whilst Mum holds the present, Suki makes a good job of tearing off the paper to reveal a bowl for her drinking water, a bowl for her food, a bag of chewy sticks, a box of biscuits and a couple of squeaky toys.

Suki is sitting and looking into Mum's eyes, her gorgeous tail continuously wagging. I have a lump in my throat seeing how happy they both are to be together.

It's just how Bella and I feel. "I think they might drive me nuts," Dad mutters as he hears the sound of a squeaky toy. Mum looks up at him with such a beautiful smile on her face. Dad continues, "There's a bag of dried food and some wet food in the garage for Suki. I didn't think you'd want to go out shopping on Christmas Day, as you have too much cooking to do," he chuckles. I can't help smiling and thinking to myself how Mum has completely forgotten about putting the potatoes on to cook. "Would my Suki like a drink in her new bowl," asks Mum, ignoring Dad's attempt at a joke. She gathers up Suki's gifts up into her arms, and heads off in the direction of the kitchen with Suki close by her side gazing up at her.

"Well I think our family is now complete," laughs Dad, giving me a big hug before we both start clearing up the wrapping paper and tags.

We listen to Mum chattering away to Suki, and I now realise where I get my chattering from. Armed with a bag of rubbish each, Dad and I go outside to the bins. Mum is now outside in the garden, and we can hear her saying "toilet Suki, come on toilet, you must need to spend a penny." Suki is sitting looking lovingly up at Mum. Dropping the rubbish quickly, I'm just in time to capture this brilliant photo.

# Chapter 16

* * *

IT'S NOW THE MIDDLE OF February and Bella's coat has turned into a mucky cream colour although it's nice and thick, I'm confused once again about the colour change as this seems to happen every year. Maybe it is just the way she is.

Bella and I have really enjoyed ourselves over the last two months, but due to the weather conditions we've been limited to where we can ride. We still manage to go to the riding school at the weekends though to practice our jumping in the sand school.

In January we had two weeks of snow but Bella wasn't bothered by it at all. I built her a snowman near the stable, I was amused as she watched me very closely in a very curious way. She was probably thinking to herself, '*I wonder what she's doing now*'. I used one of Bella's carrots for the snowman's nose and then quickly nipped back to the tack room to get a woolly hat to put on the snowman's head. I was only gone a few minutes, but on my return Bella was innocently standing eating the snowman's nose! I couldn't help but laugh. She must have thought to herself, '*Serves her right for using one of my carrots without asking*'.

I didn't bother going to get another carrot for Bella to help herself to again, we could have been there all afternoon. I just used a stick instead. I bet she thought I was a real spoil sport.

Now this is what really confused Bella. As the snow gradually started to melt, the snowman got smaller and smaller and then completely disappeared. I know Bella was more than a little concerned because she went over to where the snowman use to stand and picked up his hat. With the hat in her mouth, she looked around the paddock. I could see her thinking, *'The snowman must be here somewhere!'*

She is such a comical pony.

I did try to explain to her what had happened, but I'm not sure she completely understood. I have also promised her that if and when the snowman comes back one day, we will keep his hat ready for him. At that precise moment Bella threw the hat on the ground and walked off.

It's now the middle of March and things have got even stranger, the same as last year. Bella's coat has changed colour again, only this time it's very dark and almost chocolate in colour. She looks a totally different pony. I look on my computer at some old photographs of Bella. I have to admit I'm totally baffled as to why she has so many colour changes. I do hope eventually her colour will change back to the beautiful golden dun, but if it doesn't, it doesn't really matter, I'll always love her, whatever colour she is.

It's been a big relief not having the worry and expense of buying rugs for Bella, also she doesn't need shoes. I have read so many articles about native ponies and they all say the same. Bella doesn't need shoes, she wears her hooves down naturally. Hers are strong and tough. This is the great advantage of owning a tough and hardy New Forest pony.

# Chapter 17

* * *

TODAY IS A VERY SPECIAL day, it is Saturday 2nd April and Bella's seventh birthday.

I've been waiting patiently for Mum and Dad to go out shopping because I need to use the kitchen. I want to make Bella a carrot and pony nut birthday cake.

I pour the pony nuts into the biggest mixing bowl I can find and add six diced carrots and 10 tablespoons of molasses. I now mix it altogether with my wooden spoon. It's very hard work, more so than I'd expected. My arms are really aching and I'm not getting anywhere fast. I sigh.

Suddenly out of the corner of my eye I spot Mum's food mixer sitting invitingly on the work surface. *"This should make it a piece of cake,"* I mutter and a large grin covers my face when I realize what I've just said. I plug in the mixer and set it on the lowest setting. I switch it on, it is still such hard work and I still don't seem to be getting anywhere. Maybe it needs a bit more oomph, so I switch it to maximum power. The increase in speed is dramatic and surprising. The whisk flies out of the bowl spraying the contents all over the kitchen worktop, the windows and me. I now have molasses in my eye, and a piece of carrot on the end of my nose. If I wasn't in such a pickle this would make a great 'selfie'.

Dismayed at the awful mess, I glance at the kitchen clock and realise it's only an hour before Mum arrives back. If she sees all this, I'm going to be in big trouble.

I quickly wash my hands and face, I grab a cake tin from the cupboard, put my cake into it and bash it down flat as hard as I can with the rolling pin. It doesn't look too bad at all, and I feel quite proud of my creation. I have found a pink candle in the kitchen drawer, I stick this on the top and take a photo.

I look at the mess everywhere, I sigh and knuckle down to repair the damage and forty minutes later the kitchen looks spick and span again. Nobody would know I've used it at all. Thankfully Mum and Dad must be running late.

I've invited over Sophie and her pony Flash. Flash is a stunning nine-year-old Connemara gelding. We are going out on a birthday hack. It is now 11.00am and Sophie and Flash arrive. Bella see's Flash approaching and whinnies to him whilst can-tering up and down the paddock with her tail high in the air. She's really showing off, rearing up on her hind legs and whinnying for all she's worth. These two are really good friends, we've met up on the Downs during the winter for short rides but this is the first time Flash has come to our home.

Bella is a bit of a monkey to catch, due to her still showing off to Flash, prancing around. Sophie is no help at all. She is just sitting and laughing as I struggle to drag Bella back to the stable.

Ten minutes later and we are at last, ready to go. I've promised Mum and Dad we will be back by 4.00pm, it is only 11.30 am, so we have plenty of time.

Mum and Dad pop out to wave goodbye and Mum shouts, "Thank you for cleaning the kitchen window love. I'm not sure why you did it, but thank you." I laugh, and Sophie looks at me with a confused expression, "I'll explain later," I whisper.

I have my saddle bag, Sophie has a rucksack with sandwiches for our lunch -cucumber of course - bottled water, and I have my mobile phone. This is great. It's a clear dry day with only a slight gentle breeze.

Off we go, riding side by side through the country lanes which lead onto the South Downs. Bella is trying to kiss Flash on the way.

We always have so much to talk about. She is in hysterics as I explain to her what happened earlier whilst I was making the carrot cake, in fact she is laughing so much, for a slight second I am worried she is going to fall off Flash.

We chat about the boys at school and the ones who keep asking us out. Sophie already has a boyfriend whose name is Alan, but this doesn't stop other boys asking her out also. She's a very popular girl. Sophie and Alan have been dating for nearly a year now. I don't have a boyfriend at the moment, and to be perfectly honest I don't really want one. What with my paper round, household chores, homework and of course my gorgeous Bella, I just don't have the time or the inclination.

One or two boys have asked me out over the last few months, but to be totally honestly I prefer to spend any spare time I have with my Bella. Boys can be so boring. They always seem to be talking about football, cricket or rugby.

Soon we're up on the Downs and decide it's time to have a canter up a very steep hill. Our canter turns to a gallop; this is truly awesome and exhilarating. Bella wants to race Flash, and I have trouble holding her back. We eventually pull up at the top of the hill, and to be honest I'm completely out of breath.

"Wow!" Sophie exclaims once she's got her breath back. "That was just awesome. We definitely need to do that again soon."

We walk on for a while to let our ponies cool down.

It's now one o'clock and we decide to stop to have our sandwiches. We dismount and loosen the girths on our saddles, we push up our stirrup irons and undo the bit from the bridles. We've bought their head collars with us to put on over their bridles. We attach a lead rope and tying the reins in a knot and let the two of them graze.

*'How wonderful is this'*, I think to myself but once again say it out loud.

The grass is still damp so our ponies will take in the water from the fresh lush grass as they graze. I compliment Sophie on my sandwiches and phone Mum to tell her we're all fine. We are now ready to continue on our ride.

We head towards the woods. Bella really enjoys it here. We canter a few strides behind Flash, Sophie turns her head and shouts, "There's a fallen tree up ahead we can jump."

It's quite dark in certain areas where the trees are bunched together. We clear another log and another nice jump from Bella. We pull our ponies up and discuss which path we are going to take.

I can sense Bella is feeling very excited now and she is cantering on the spot. She leaps forward putting in a little buck. I've got use to these now, and I now know exactly when the bucks are coming, well most of the time anyway!

We continue through the woods, jumping fallen trees and anything else lying around which will make a good jump. I nearly fall off as we jump a log lying on the ground. The jump is fine but branches of a nearby tree are hanging low, and I don't see them in time to duck. They hit me full in the face! '*Ouch!*' I shout.

Sophie calls, "Emily, are you ok?"

"I'm fine," I shout back. "I just got smacked in the face by a branch."

Her very unhelpful response is, "You're always saying how much you want to branch out Emily. Well, you've just taken your first step." Sophie has such a great sense of humour and I nearly fall off again, due to laughing so much.

At the far end of the woods it is dark and shady, the temperature seems to have dropped and the ground underneath is muddy and slippery. We decide to get off our ponies and lead them.

There are a few puddles and Bella is in her element. She splashes and splashes away covering my jodhpurs in dirty wet mud, much to Sophie's amusement.

"Oh Bella, what are you like?" I mutter trying to wipe the cold, stodgy mud from my jodhpurs. Sophie laughs even more, but at this precise moment Flash decides to splash in the puddles too. Sophie's shocked face makes me laugh out loud as she looks down at her - what were - nice beige jodhpurs are now in fact two-tone in colour. Luckily for me my jodhpurs are black. "Serves you right for laughing at me Sophie," I shout back at her.

We continue walking on foot until we reach the top end of the woods. What a beautiful view of the village of Berwick, which is around two miles from home. I know I'll never tire of looking at this stunning scenery.

Remounting our ponies, we follow the bridleway through three fields and eventually come out near the village. We decide to continue riding through the fields as they are nice and level and glancing at my watch I see it is 2.30 pm so we have plenty of time to get home.

# Chapter 18

WE RIDE SIDE BY SIDE being careful not to ride on any of the Farmers crops as we merrily chat away.

"Sophie, ever since I've had Bella, I've had a problem with her mane. I brush it over so it falls nicely on her offside but then it bounces back onto her nearside. I've tried dampening it every night but as soon as Bella shakes her head, it's back to square one. I want to take her to her first show in August, and I just know we'll lose points if her mane doesn't fall the right way. Do you have any tips?" I ask her.

"Why don't you plait her mane? I've heard this works," suggests Sophie. "If I were you, I'd certainly give it a try. This show in August, where is it?"

"Mrs Evans, is organising a big show this year at the riding school. It's on August 15th. Why do you ask? Are you interested?" "Well if you and Bella are going, then I might be," replies Sophie.

"I have an idea," I grin at her. "I could ask Mum and Dad if you and Flash can stay over at ours. Bella and Flash could stay in the paddock together overnight, we could get them ready early in the morning and ride over together. What do you think?"

"Brilliant," screeches Sophie. "I'll ask Mum and Dad when I get home and will text you later. We could have a midnight feast out in the paddock, and chat for hours. Oh Emily, this is going to be great fun," she replies beaming at me.

"I know," I reply starting to feel excited myself. "We could put our tent up and sleep in the paddock with Flash and Bella." "Wow, I could bring my sleeping bag over too!" cries Sophie.

Just as we're beginning to make plans, a little brown dog appears from nowhere, and starts barking continuously at us.

Flash jumps in surprise but Bella stops instantly and puts her head down to look closely at him.

"Hello, little dog, where are you from? Have you got lost? Are you a long way from home?" I ask in a very quiet voice.

Dismounting, I stoop down next to the little dog. He whines as I slowly look at the disc on his collar. "Pear Shape Cottage, Berwick," I read out loud to Sophie. "I'm sure that's at the bottom end of the village, by the post office."

The little dog starts barking again, and turns and runs to the edge of the next field, he stops and looks directly at us barking madly. I jump back on Bella and wonder why he's acting so strange.

"Maybe he just got out and ran off," suggests Sophie.

By now the dog is standing beside a nearby hedge. He's barking louder than ever, and wagging his tail. As we approach, we both gasp at what we see. Lying on the ground in front of the hedge, is an elderly lady.

Both Sophie and I jump off our ponies as fast as we can. Sophie holds both sets of reins and I rush over to see if the old lady is moving. She's lying very still. Moving closer I whisper "Hello, are you OK?"

The old lady makes a groaning noise, and manages to mumble, "My leg. My head."

"She's alive," I call to Sophie. "Hand me your coat and I'll use mine too, these will help to warm her up a little. She looks and feels very cold. Will you get my phone from my saddle bag and I'll call for an ambulance."

Sophie hands me my mobile phone and I dial 999.

"Ambulance, fire or police?" the operator asks.

"Ambulance please."

"How can I help you?" asks a gentleman on the other end of the phone.

"My friend and I are out riding our ponies, and we've found an elderly lady lying by a hedge. She must have had a bad fall. She's managed to tell me that her leg and her head hurt."

"Where are you?" he asks.

"The second field at the back of the old school," I reply.

"I don't think an ambulance will be able to get over to her, unless the fields are dry."

"They are quite stodgy," I admit.

After a couple of minutes talking, I suggest that I ride over to meet the ambulance outside the old school, and then the crew can follow me back on foot to the old lady. We decide it's better for Sophie to stay with the old lady and her dog, and most importantly keep talking to her and keep her awake.

I vault onto Bella, surprising myself. I'm so proud and chuffed that I have managed to do this at last but for now I need to focus. We gallop across two fields as fast as we can in the direction of the old school house. Bella is very well behaved, and I'm sure she's sensing that we're on an important mission. She responds eagerly, and does everything I ask of her.

The fields we're riding through seem endless, although it's probably only been a few minutes and eventually we arrive at the playing field at the back of the old school house. I'm out of breath and Bella is blowing hard too, Dismounting, I lead her through the gate and around to the front of the building to wait for the ambulance.

A few minutes later I hear the siren in the distance but then it goes silent. Suddenly, the ambulance comes into view. To be honest, I have been secretly worried as to how Bella would respond to the loud siren but the ambulance crew must have thought of this, and turned off the siren before they came too close. I can now stop worrying and get back to the job in hand.

The driver of the ambulance jumps out quickly, and with his colleague they both follow me to the back of the school house, where I point out in the far distance where the lady is.

The driver pushes his boot into the mud to test the ground then says, "There's no way the ambulance will be able to get over there. It'll get stuck for sure."

They both return to the ambulance, and return quickly carrying two bags and a stretcher. Mounting Bella, I reach out for one of their bags and put it over my shoulder. The driver is very grateful, and they follow closely behind as Bella and I walk on.

At last we reach the old lady who is now sitting up. She has a nasty gash on her head and informs the ambulance men, she can't move her right ankle.

Slowly and carefully her right wellington boot is cut off with a giant pair of scissors. Her ankle is very swollen and bruised, and they suspect it's broken.

"We'll have to take you to the hospital for x-rays," one of the ambulance men informs her.

Carefully they help her to stand up and try to steady her as she hops about desperately trying to get her balance, not daring to put her other painful leg on the ground.

The elderly lady, whose name turns out to be Mrs James, is adamant she's not going to be carried on a stretcher. She's very stubborn.

Whilst we'd been gone Sophie had been chatting with Mrs James who apparently up until the age of seventy two had still been riding horses. She's travelled the world schooling ponies but had to stop riding due to her eye sight deteriorating, and she has arthritis in her spine.

As the ambulance men stand scratching their heads trying to think of a way they are going to get this stubborn elderly lady back, Sophie pipes up with a great idea, "As Mrs James is refusing to be carried on a stretcher, maybe the solution is for her to ride one of our ponies back?"

Mrs James responds quicker than any of us, "Oh yes please, can I? I won't feel so silly then."

"I don't think we have much choice," says one of the ambulance men in a very reluctant tone.

We decide it will be safer for Mrs James to ride Bella, with me leading her.

The ambulance driver gently lifts her onto Bella's back. She gasps in pain but blurts out, "I'm fine, I can cope, please stop fussing."

I smile at her and think what a lovely lady she is. Bella is behaving very well as we slowly walk through the stodgy fields. I'm so proud of her.

"What a beautiful pony you have here young lady," praises Mrs James. "When I'm better, maybe I can come and see you ride her at your home. I can't thank you and Sophie enough for all you've done. If you hadn't found me, I hate to think what would have happened to me out there in the dark all night."

"Well it was your little dog who alerted us and showed us where you were," I reply, turning to look at Sophie.

# Chapter 19

$*$  $*$  $*$

SOPHIE IS FOLLOWING CLOSELY BEHIND on Flash, carrying the little dog whose name we now know is Toddy. He looks to be really enjoying himself and apparently this is his first time riding a horse. Mrs James had told Sophie her daughter has owned the post office in the village for the last 20 years and asks us if we would be kind enough to let her know what has happened and to take Toddy there for her to look after. We both agree and tell her this will be no problem.

Eventually we arrive at the old school house and the ambulance men virtually lift Mrs James off Bella as if she is as light as a feather. Mrs James turns to me and Sophie, "You seriously cannot believe how happy and thrilled I am to have sat on a pony again after all these years, thank you". She smiles at us, kisses Toddy and is helped into the ambulance. We wish her well and wave the ambulance off and glancing at my watch I see that it's 4.05pm. "Oh no," I gasp. "I'd better phone Mum; she'll be worrying." I find my phone and quickly to explain to Mum what's happened and tell her we'll be back as soon as we've dropped Toddy off at the post office.

Mrs James's daughter is a very lovely lady too. She is totally shocked as we explain to her what has happened and she can't thank us enough. "Once I have settled Toddy in and he has eaten his dinner, I will go straight to the hospital" she informs us as she continues to stroke Toddy and tell him what a clever, intelligent dog he is, and a hero for alerting us to his Mum's accident. He licks her hands affectionately.

"What a bizarre old day," I sigh to Sophie, as we set off home.

Sophie decides she'd better go straight home, "I'll text you later," she calls as she waves goodbye.

Mum is waiting for me by the gate. I'm talking nineteen to the dozen, hardly stopping to take a breath as I tell her all about our adventure whilst un-tacking Bella and getting her feed ready. Mum listens eagerly, she's so proud of all of us, especially Toddy. "How sensible you've all been," says Mum, proudly giving me a massive hug.

What an eventful day on Bella's birthday!

It is now 7.00pm and time to give Bella her birthday cake, and an extra big cuddle. She is loving her cake and licking her lips, and is trying to eat it all but I decide it's only fair to save some cake for Flash. I kiss Bella goodnight and gallop back to the bungalow.

The phone is ringing as I enter the kitchen, and Mum rushes to answer it. Mrs James is calling from the hospital to thank us all again. Mum puts her on loud speaker. Mrs James informs us she has a broken ankle which is now in plaster and she's going to have to stay in hospital overnight. She has tried arguing with the nurses, telling them she would be better off at home, but the doctor insists she has to stay in overnight to keep a close eye on her in case she has concussion. After 10 minutes or so of continuous talking on Mrs James part, probably the drugs she's on for the pain I think to myself, she finishes off by saying that she can't wait to get home to give her gorgeous dog Toddy a big hug as she is missing him dearly. This will be the first night they have ever spent apart. Mum smiles at me, she hasn't had much chance to say a word.

# Chapter 20

* * *

I'M SO EXHAUSTED IT DOESN'T take long before I'm in a deep sleep. It feels like I've only just dropped off when I'm rudely awoken again.

Argh! Beep, beep, beep. Here we go again I think as I jump out of bed. I suddenly remember our adventure from yesterday. What an exciting day we all had. A little worrying, but totally unexpected at the same time.

When I return from my paper round, Mum shouts to me, "Emily, the local press have telephoned to ask if they can come along and take photos of the five heroes. Mrs James and her dog Toddy will also be coming."

"Wow!" I can hardly believe it.

Sophie, and Flash, arrive at one o'clock, and at two o'clock the photographer rolls up in a battered old van. Ten minutes later, Mrs James arrives. She is struggling to get the hang of using a pair of crutches and is aided by her daughter. Mrs James looks fine apart from a nasty bruise on her cheek and a plaster cast on her right ankle. Toddy is jumping around, wagging his tail and barking in excitement.

Wondering what all the excitement is about, Suki comes running out of the bungalow. Toddy and Suki sniff each other warily at first, but then have a great game running after each other playing tag. Another new friend for Suki. It's great as she really is starting to enjoy her new life now.

Click, click, photographs are taken with us on our ponies with Mrs James and Toddy standing in between me and Sophie.

The photographer is at last finished; he checks to make sure he is happy with the images. Mum asks Mrs James, her daughter and the photographer if they would like to come into the bungalow for a drink. The photographer declines, saying he has to get back to the office as he has a deadline to meet and he heads off back to his van.

Sophie and I untack Flash and Bella, and let them out into the paddock. We watch as they have great fun chasing each other around before eventually deciding to settle down to eat grass. We make our way back to the kitchen to find Toddy now has his own special bowl of fresh water to drink and Mum is fussing over him, stroking him, cuddling him, and telling him what a gorgeous clever boy he is over and over again. Toddy is loving every second of the fuss he's getting and Mum is making sure Suki isn't feeling left out as she fusses over her too.

An hour has flown by and Mrs James, her daughter and Toddy have to leave to go home. Mrs James has to take things easy for the time being, and mustn't get tired out. We wave them off with Mrs James shouting to us she will be in touch very soon.

As we walk back inside, I ask Mum whether Sophie can come to stay for one night on the fourteenth of August. I tell her all about the show. Sophie informs me, she has just found out her parents are away on holiday that week and she may have to go and stay with her Nan.

"Why don't I ask your parents if you and Flash can come and stay for the whole week?" Mum blurts out much to our surprise.

"Oh, yes, please!" Sophie and I scream at exactly the same time.

\* \* \*

It is now Wednesday and the local paper is out, the headline reads;

## 'TWO LOCAL GIRLS AND THEIR PONIES IN A REMARKABLE RESCUE'

Our families and friends are really proud of us. Mrs Evans also calls to congratulate us and one week later Sophie and I are invited to the Mayor's office. We are thrilled to be there with our parents. We're presented with a community award from the Mayor for our wonderful achievement, this really was a very special moment. Bella and Flash received a large bag of carrots. Toddy received a squeaky dog toy to enjoy as he played the major part in alerting us to his mistress's accident. Can you believe I was served cucumber sandwiches with no crusts!

\* \* \*

It's soon the month of May and Bella has turned back into a golden dun colour. I'm secretly quite relieved!

A favourite part of my daily routine is grooming her, and I'm amazed at how much hair I've brushed out of Bella during the last three weeks.

I'll love Bella whatever colour she is but this golden dun colour is so pretty and stunning when the sun shines on her soft, gleaming coat.

Her mane now falls the right way. Mrs James kindly came over to see us two weeks ago and spent a few hours teaching me how to plait properly. Here is a photo I took after we had finished putting in her trendy plaits. This really had been very kind and thoughtful of Mrs James. Toddy came too but he spent most of the time being spoilt by Mum and enjoying running around and playing games with Suki.

How funny it was taking Bella's plaits out one week later. Her mane had turned so curly! Mrs James certainly has a lot of knowledge of horses and ponies and has told me if I need any help in the future with Bella to just ask as she would be honoured to help. She is also coming to the show in August to cheer us on.

Only ten weeks to go, and Sophie and Flash will be coming to stay. We will be going to our very first show. I can't help but smile as I think about how much fun we are going to have.

# Chapter 21

* * *

TODAY IS THE 7TH AUGUST, the day before my 16th birthday. It's nearly a year since my dream pony Bella came to live here, and what wonderful times we've spent together.

I'm also excited as Mum and Dad have arranged a birthday party for me. Twenty of my friends together with all of my family are coming. Dad is doing a barbecue and has a friend who is going to do a disco. This is all going to take place in our garden as long as the weather allows. Luckily, the forecast is clear, dry, and sunny.

I've explained to Bella what will be going on and I have told her she must not be frightened of the loud music and if she is, I won't be far away and will be checking on her regularly.

Over the last three weeks, I've been leaving my CD player on for a couple of hours when Bella is in her stable. She really seems to like Elvis Presley. Good taste this pony. I swear she's trying to dance in her stable as she curls up her lip to Jailhouse Rock. I have tried so many times to creep up to the stable door to catch her in the act but every time I put my head over the stable door, she is standing still looking at me in a very comical and mischievous way. Maybe it is just my imagination.

No need for my alarm today, I'm wide awake at 5.30am. Jumping out of bed I run straight across to my window and throw back the curtains. The sun is brightly shining for my birthday, and it's going to be a clear dry day for my party.

I quickly wash and dress and let myself out of the back door as quietly as a mouse so as not to wake Mum and Dad and head straight out to Bella.

"Good morning Bella," I call to her as I fetch her breakfast. "Do you realise it's one year ago today that you came to live here. We've had such fun haven't we?"

Bella tucks into her breakfast only occasionally lifting her head to look at me with those gorgeous eyes. I know she's listening to me because her ears are moving backwards and forwards. "I'll be back soon, but now I have to go and do my paper round."

I deliver the newspapers as fast as possible, probably in record time. I can't help but wonder what presents will be waiting for me when I get home.

I need to make sure I have the correct riding clothes for Bella's first show which is now only one week away.

I've seen a second-hand show jacket at the local saddlery which is priced at £25, it's a lovely shade of brown, and just what I need. I also need white or cream jodhpurs; new ones are priced at £50 but I've seen a second hand pair for £10 and these will do just as well. I need a white shirt as well, plus a tie and hair net. All of this will cost £55 in total. My mind is flitting from one topic to another. I'm just so excited with everything at the moment.

Up until now I've saved £70, and with the £650 still in Bella's bucket, it's totting up nicely. I never break into Bella's bucket unless I have to. I call this her 'emergency pot' and is used for injections, and anything else she needs. Having just renewed Bella's insurance for another year, I'm very pleased with my finances.

Finally, I arrive home and head straight for the kitchen. Mum is singing along to her favourite CD of Michael Buble', "All I do is dream of you, the whole night through," she bellows at the top of her voice shaking her hips at the same time. Tip-toing in as quietly as I can, I creep up behind her. She's now happily folding the washing; I tap her on the right shoulder and step to the left so when she looks around she can't see me straight away. Mum jumps high in the air screaming, and drops the washing onto the floor before she sees it's only me. Suki also jumps and barks at the same time.

"Oooh, you little so and so," Mum splutters laughing at the same time. "Happy 16th Birthday love, come here and give me a big hug, and a big, big kiss".

Assuming I must be home, judging by the noise and commotion coming from the kitchen, Dad appears in the doorway carrying presents and cards. "Hello Emily. Happy Birthday love. Come here and give me a hug, then you can then open your presents and cards," he says as he walks across to place them on the table.

I give Dad a big hug and a kiss and the three of us sit down to drink the coffee Mum has placed there only minutes before. She knows my routine backwards by now, and how long it takes me to do my round and get back home.

I eagerly open my presents and I am thrilled to see I have a pair of cream jodhpurs from one Nan and Grandad. These are a perfect fit, probably thanks to mum again.

My other Nan and Grandad have given me money which is fabulous as I can put this towards purchasing a black velvet riding hat that I have been drooling over. Aunty Lynette and family have sent a gift of a perfect white shirt; Aunty Sharon and Uncle Gary have enclosed a voucher for the local saddlery inside my birthday card and I will use this to get some Jodhpur boots. What fantastic presents! How lucky am I?

"Our present isn't on the table as you can see love," explains Dad. "We've arranged, and paid for a horse box to take you and Bella down to Devon next Easter in the school holidays. You'll be able to have a lovely break and enjoy lots of fun with your Aunty Pam."

"OMG, really, are you serious? Thank you, thank you, what a totally awesome present," I shriek, as I jump up to hug them both.

Aunty Pam, Dad's sister, is a very horsey person. She owns two horses and competes in dressage competitions. She also rescues ponies and has ten at her home at the moment. I always love listening to the stories she tells me, although sometimes they can be very sad. I've always wanted to visit her but just couldn't bear the thought of leaving Bella. Now I don't have to, because she will be coming with me.

Aunty Pam and I email each other regularly and sometimes skype. We've always got on really well, possibly because we have so much in common and always so much to talk about.

Maybe Bella and I will pick up some tips on how to do dressage. Although I really can't wait to help out with the rescue ponies.

I'm so excited and can't wait to tell Bella all about our holiday. This will be around the time of Bella's birthday. I have always dreamt of riding along a sandy beach and my dream could now come true with my dream pony Bella. Finishing my toast and the rest of my coffee, I thank Mum and Dad again and gallop out to tell Bella the brilliant news.

Pinned to the fence on the outside of the paddock is a card which has a photo of Bella and myself on the front. The card reads, '*To my mummy xxx*'.

Just below this is a present lying on the ground. I feel a lump in my throat. This is so sweet. I open the card to see a hoof print imbedded there. Bella has remembered my birthday!

Climbing through the fence, I reach up and give Bella a big hug and a kiss on her soft warm muzzle. I bend down to pick up the present, Bella cheekily grabs the wrapping paper and grips it tightly in her mouth. I try and pull it back, the paper rips and a box falls to the ground. Bella is standing looking at me. I can see her thinking '*Oh dear*'. She turns around swiftly, the paper still hanging from her mouth, and canters proudly around the field holding her tail very high in the air.

I can't help myself and collapse in a fit of giggles. She is such a funny girl. Eventually Bella stops cantering and walks calmly back towards me. She stops a short distance away and once again is looking at me. She now decides to drop the wrapping paper into her water bucket!

I stoop down to pick up the box from the ground and I'm thankful to see it isn't damaged. Bella could quite easily have trodden on it when she took off cantering away across the paddock. I open it eagerly and I am thrilled to find a pair of dark blue waterproof trousers. "Awesome Bella, thank you. These are just what I need for the winter months," I grin at her.

# Chapter 22

* * *

TODAY OUR HOME IS A hive of activity. Aunty Lynette and Aunty Sharon have come over to help prepare the food ready for my party. Mum has asked everyone to bring certain food items, loaves of bread, quiches, sausage rolls, peanuts, crisps, etc. My cousins Amy, Chris and Martin have come over too. I offer to help make the sandwiches, but thankfully Mum declines and informs my cousins to take me out from under her feet and go and play outside. We don't need telling twice, and head outside as fast as we can before Mum changes her mind.

We decide to have a game of football in the paddock and Bella finds this very entertaining. At first she snorts loudly at what she assumes is a round object moving around on its own, and as it moves towards her she gallops off with her tail high in the air.

"What a big baby you are Bella," laughs Martin.

Bella doesn't like the fact she is missing out, and after a few minutes bravely comes across to have another look at the ball. She paws it with her near foreleg, looking completely baffled as to where it has gone. In fact it shot through her back legs, but Bella is still looking for the ball to her left, to her right and straight ahead, she still hasn't realised it is behind her.

"I don't think you'll make a footballer, Bella." Martin chuckles.

We all have a quick snack at lunchtime followed by a game of hide and seek. Bella thinks this is a very amusing game, and she is not helping me at all. Every time I try to hide she follows me giving my hiding place away, and I'm out quickly much to everyone's amusement.

It is now 5.00pm and time for me to get ready for the party. I decide to put Bella in the front yard, so she can see everything that's going on. I leave her stable open in case tonight's events get a bit too much for her, she can then pop off to bed if she wants to.

I am excited about dressing up in my disco clothes. I tie my hair up in what I feel is the latest fashion with a hand- made bobble in the shape of a horse's head, and decide to put on some lipstick - something I very rarely do. I look at myself in the long mirror in the hallway, and I'm very pleased with the way I look. *'Wow, is that really me?'* I say to myself as I continue to admire myself at every angle possible. I don't get dressed up very often, as I much prefer to run around in my 'pony clothes'.

Outside I can hear the music blaring, I hadn't realised the disco was already here. I try to gallop out to the yard but soon realise this is not an easy task with these party shoes on and I have to slow down to a trot and then a walk. I'm worried Bella might be scared of the loud music but to my surprise she's standing very relaxed at the fence, ears pricked forward and is watching everything with great interest. I give her a pat on her neck, and kiss her and as I leave, I shout over my shoulder, "See you shortly Bella, love you."

Dad is busy getting the barbecue going, and before too long the smell of sizzling sausages is making my mouth water and my belly rumble. I'm a vegetarian by choice, and very much looking forward to my veggie sausages that I've been promised, and not forgetting a delicious chip butty.

# Chapter 23

* * *

Soon our home is buzzing with so many people. I smile as I look around, some of my friends are chatting, some are eating and others are dancing.

Suddenly, 'Uptown Funk' starts playing, and I have an uncontrollable feeling that I must dance, or I will burst. I just love Bruno Mars. I really can't help myself as I start to boogie. I am not sure what my dancing looks like but I don't care, I am having so much fun. I dance and dance and dance and I'm definitely glowing. My Nan once told me that it's un-lady like to say you are dripping with sweat, even if you are! You should say you are glowing instead as it sounds so much nicer. Well at this precise moment I must look like a flashing beacon.

What a brilliant party this is! 'I Will Always Love You' is now playing, another of my favourite singers, Whitney Houston. A boy from school called Simon is walking directly towards me, "Emily, would you do me the honour of dancing with me" he asks in a very polite voice. I nod although I do feel a little self-conscious, but as I look around I see a lot of other couples dancing, so I relax and enjoy myself.

Mum and Dad are also dancing, but halfway through the song someone shouts out to Dad that his sausages are burning! He runs off quickly on a mission to save his sausages. Mum jogs off after him but moments later appears with Suki in her arms, and finishes the dance with her. Suki seems to be enjoying herself too, and Mum can hardly see where she's going because her little dog just keeps licking her face.

The song has stopped and I ask Simon if he would like to meet Bella. "I would love to" he replies. We walk and talk and he tells me he actually has his own pony who is called Thunder. "Maybe we can meet up for a ride one day?" he is asking me. "That would be lovely" I reply.

As we make our way across to Bella she is looking straight at us in a very comical way. She lets out a little whinny. "Emily, Bella is very pretty, just like you, her owner", blurts out Simon, I turn my head away as I can feel myself blushing. I must really be glowing right now!

Thankfully Sophie and Alan come to join us, just in the nick of time I think to myself. Sophie, Alan and Simon already know each other, so the four of us sit down on the stable yard floor chatting away with Bella standing just behind me. Bella soon gets bored of listening to all the chatter, and saunters into her stable. I'm sure she thinks it is time to liven things up. I can hear her having a long drink of water, she comes back out, stands behind Simon, and slowly dribbles water down the back of his neck!

We all burst out laughing, and Bella curls her top lip in the air like she's also joining in too. I bet she is thinking, *'This is a result, I feel like I am really part of the 'gang' now!'*

Mum is calling me, "Time to sing Happy Birthday and cut your cake Emily, hurry up."

We quickly return to the garden and everyone sings Happy Birthday to me. I take a deep breath and manage to blow all 16 candles out in one go.

"Make a wish Emily," says Dad.

I close my eyes and wish hard and long. *'I wish, I wish Bella and I do well at the show next week, and win a rosette '*. Everyone cheers and claps as I cut my birthday cake.

All too soon it is 11.00pm, and time for everyone to leave and go home. I change into some flat shoes and gallop across to the stable to put Bella to bed only to find her playing with a stray balloon. As she looks in my direction, her hoof catches the balloon in just the right place and it pops loudly. She jumps backwards and looks all around for her balloon. She can't seem to understand where it's gone, and that the flat piece of rubber on the floor is the remains of what's left of her balloon! A bit like the snowman.

"I don't know," I say to her picking the rubber up off the ground and showing it to her. "It's a good job I came when I did because if you'd eaten this you could have choked."

I lead Bella into her stable and wish her goodnight, I can see she's exhausted. "You're tired out after watching everything aren't you? You just lie down and have a good night's sleep and I will see you in the morning, love you my Bella." I leave her to settle herself down, turn off the lights, and blow her a kiss like I do every night.

Back at the bungalow, I muck in helping Mum and Dad clear up, and bless Sophie and Alan, they have stayed to help too. Soon the outside is cleared. All the rubbish has been bagged up so nothing can blow into Bella's paddocks, and the rest can be done in the morning.

"Night," Sophie shouts to me as she heads off home down the path. "See you real soon, I can't wait to come and stay."

"Me too," I shout back. "Thanks for your help." It's now definite that Sophie and Flash, will be coming to stay for a week. I cannot wait. I am so looking forward to it.

Returning inside with Mum and Dad, I thank them for a wonderful party. I'm absolutely exhausted, it's now 1.00am in the morning, but I have had a truly amazing 16th birthday.

At least I don't have to rush to do my paper round in the morning I remember as I open my mouth letting out a huge yawn. I've been given the morning off.

Getting into my pyjamas I jump into bed and let out another big yawn. I fall fast asleep as soon as my head touches the pillow.

# Chapter 24

$*\quad*\quad*$

I WAKE UP, AND SIT bolt upright, I'm sure I can hear a whinny very close by. Rubbing my eyes, I follow the sound which seems to be coming from my bedroom window. I'd left it open last night as it was so warm. I am surprised to see Bella's head sticking through it, gazing across at me. How did this happen? I am sure I tucked her up in bed in the early hours.

"What are you doing here?" I gasp, quickly jumping out of bed and walking across to her.

At this precise moment Mum comes walking into my bedroom. "Morning, Emily. I hope you don't mind love, but your dad fed Bella at seven o'clock this morning, and put her out in her paddock."

Looking at my watch I'm astounded to see it is 11.00am. "Oh no, my paper round!" I gasp. Panic stricken I start to dash off and get ready, but Mum manages to grab my arm and stop me.

"It's alright Emily, dear," soothes Mum. Don't you remember? You have the morning off."

"Oh, what a relief, that's good," and giving a big sigh, I sink back down onto my bed. "I must thank Dad when I see him. That was really kind of him, the excitement of my birthday must have whacked me out."

"I bet now Bella knows where you sleep, she'll come to your window more often," says Mum with a grin.

I tell Bella to go and eat some grass as I need to get washed and dressed but this is a complete waste of time, she thinks it's much more fun to pull at my bedroom curtains. She has one half of the curtains in her mouth and is tugging it. The curtain moves sideways which makes her jump, and snorting she lets it drop. "Serves you right," I say sternly. Mum just laughs at her antics.

Mum thinks it would be wise to tuck the curtains up over the curtain rail, so they're out of the way of a very curious Bella. Bella soon gets fed up at being ignored, and walks away sulkily.

After getting washed and dressed and having a quick breakfast, I help Mum and Dad tidy the inside of the bungalow. It's still in a bit of a mess from last night's party. Once everything is back to normal and cleared away, Dad goes up into the loft to get the tent down. We will need this for Sophie and Flash's arrival tomorrow.

Sophie, and I have already decided that Bella and Flash will stay out in the paddock together over night, and in the stable yard area with the stable left open during the day. This should work quite well, as long as they don't get up to too much mischief.

# Chapter 25

$*$ $*$ $*$

IT IS 10.00AM IN THE morning and at last the 10th August is here and Sophie has just arrived with Flash. Her parents have followed her in their car with her two large suitcases in the boot.

"I'm always in two minds what to wear, so I've come prepared," explains Sophie.

"It's only a week you know," I answer back, giggling.

"I know Emily but all my show clothes are in the medium suitcase and in the larger one there is a mixture of this and that. I thought it best to be prepared. Plus there's my iPad and make up."

Jumping off Flash, Sophie walks over to kiss her mum and dad goodbye, and wishes them a lovely holiday.

Mum and Dad have come out to greet them, and they all have a quick few words.

"Now you behave yourself, and have a good time. Good luck at the show too," says Sophie's Mum, her Dad just grins at his daughter. They return to their car, wave their goodbyes, and leave for the airport to catch their plane to Greece.

Bella calls to Flash, and Flash whinnies back.

"Let's get them settled first, then after lunch we can put the tent up," I suggest. "Also will you remind me later that I still need to pick up my show jacket during the week? I've phoned the Saddlery and they're definitely saving it for me."

"I'll try to remember," laughs Sophie.

Sophie untacks Flash, and leads him out to the field so he can be with Bella. The two of them gallop off to the other end of the paddock, swing around and come galloping back. We are both standing watching their antics, I am holding my breath, they're going too fast, and it looks as if they are going to crash through the fencing.

Thankfully at the last minute they both swerve off in the opposite direction and gallop back to the other end of the field. My heart is beating ten to the dozen.

"Phew that was close!" I gasp. We wait a little longer to make sure they have settled down and at last we can leave them grazing peacefully, and go inside to have something to eat ourselves.

It's a good job I've already cleared half of my wardrobe out as Sophie needs a lot of hanging space to put her clothes!

After lunch Sophie finishes unpacking, and puts Flash's veterinary certificate with Bella's. We need these to show that our ponies' flu and tetanus jabs are up to date for the show on Sunday. Bella's yearly booster was done last month.

Flash, according to his veterinary certificate is short for 'Flash The Silver Dancer.'

"What a posh name. Maybe I should give Bella a posh name too. I know, how about Chatterbox Bella?" "I think that's too much like your nickname Emily, Chatterbox Emily!" replies Sophie. "You need something a little more sophisticated, a bit more lady like."

We both try to think of a suitable name but can only come up with ridiculous names, or names that wouldn't be suitable like, Champagne Bella, Crazy Bella, Cranky Bella, Calypso Bella, Dancing Ballerina, or Barmy Bella. Eventually we have to give up. Our sides are aching so much from laughing.

It is now time to bath our ponies. Gathering together all the items we need, shampoo, buckets, sponges, and sweat scraper, we head over to the paddock. Bella is stretched out fast asleep in the sunshine, with Flash standing looking over her as if he's protecting her. They look so cute together. Sophie quickly takes a photo on her iPhone.

"Who shall we tackle first?" I ask.

"Well, we'd better do Bella I think, she has more stains on her than Flash!"

We walk up to our ponies, put on their head collars and head back to the stable yard. After tying them up securely, I walk to the bungalow with the empty buckets, and return walking much slower, with two heavy buckets containing three quarters full of lovely warm water as I try very hard not to slosh it down my legs. Although there is a water tap by Bella's stable, only cold water flows from it, using warm water first will help to wash the worst of the stains off Bella's coat.

Bella stands patiently whilst we sponge her thoroughly all over. Flash is being a bit of a nuisance insisting on nibbling Bella's legs, so we agree enough is enough, and move him into the stable out of the way, much to his disgust!

Once Bella is nicely soaked we're ready for the shampoo. Working really hard, and producing a nice thick lather, we give her a good old massage at the same time. Next comes the rinsing. This time we can use the hose attached to the tap which makes it a lot easier to wash the soap away. We soon realise we've been a bit too enthusiastic with the shampoo and it takes quite some time to rinse it all out, due to the bubbles disappearing and reappearing. Working from her neck downwards using the sweat scraper, we continue until we have removed as much water as we physically can.

Now, time to wash her tail. It's quite a job trying to fit it all into the bucket of warm water, there's so much of it. Sophie holds the bucket up as high as her arms will allow, and I stuff as much of Bella's tail in as I possibly can. I splash the water up to the top so it's all nicely soaked, then place the bucket back onto the ground, off I go with the shampoo again, taking care not to use too much this time.

"It's like washing out a dish cloth isn't it," giggles Sophie, as she watches me rubbing her tail between my hands. Now time for the rinse. Bella turns her head to watch now and again and I must say how good she is being, standing quietly and being very patient. She really seems to be enjoying all this pampering, either that, or she's quietly thinking what mischief she can get up to when we have finished. I grab the hose again and continue rinsing until the water runs clear. I wring out her tail holding it in one hand, I swing it in a circle as fast as I can to get as much water out as possible, then let it fall gently. Bella must like this sensation as she suddenly gives her tail an almighty swish. Unfortunately, I haven't moved out of the way and end up being smacked across the face with a wet tail. This sets Sophie off in fits of giggles. It really was quite a whack, and my cheeks tingle like mad.

Now to start the process all over again with Flash. He too seems to enjoy himself but is quite fidgety. A couple of times he knocks over the buckets of water which is very frustrating. Eventually he is finished and we let out huge sighs of relief. What a long job this has turned out to be, but well worth it. They both look gorgeous.

By now the sun is very hot, so we take our ponies out in the paddock so they can dry off properly, and stretch their legs.

This turns out to be a very bad idea, as soon as we let them both go, the first thing they do is to get down to have a jolly good old roll!

"Charming," we both say in unison, and stand with our hands on our hips watching in disgust as the dust flies everywhere.

"We'll have to remember not to do that ever again!" exclaims Sophie. "Next time they can stay in the yard until they're dry."

Slowly we walk back to the kitchen to get a drink. We both manage to drink two large glasses of cold water. We're so thirsty after all our hard work. We relax for twenty minutes laying on the grass, the sun is shining beautifully, we don't really want to get up but we need to bring our mischievous ponies back into the yard.

Now it is time to put up the tent. I glance at my watch, 3.00pm. This also turns out to be harder than we anticipated but finally after three attempts the tent is erected and we stand back to admire our handiwork.

We let out another huge sigh of relief.

We have set the tent up outside my bedroom window, in hindsight this turns out to be another bad idea! At 7.00pm after dinner we pop out to feed our ponies and let them out for the night into the paddock. Without thinking, we release them out into the first paddock which yes, contains our tent.

Flash and Bella canter straight across to the big green tent and start prancing around, snorting, their eyes are wide open in amazement. Bella must think there's an intruder in her paddock and is kicking out at the tent in disgust with her hind legs. She continues kicking the tent as if she is really trying to kill it. Sophie and I run across as quickly as we can to try and salvage the tent, and find a large rip down one side.

"Oh no," I groan. "Now what are we going to do?"

Bella and Flash are cantering around the paddock with their tails held high, still snorting and prancing.

"They might be naughty ponies, but what lovely little movers they are. Sophie, Flash is doing some awesome dressage moves" I say admiringly.

"We'll have to take the tent down, or move our ponies into the other paddock," replies Sophie. "But we can't put them in the other paddock because the grass is too rich for them to spend the whole night in." I let out a huge sigh, "We'll have to take the tent down and sleep inside tonight."

Hearing all the commotion, Mum and Dad are rushing over to see what's going on. We explain what has happened and Mum can't stop laughing.

"What mischievous ponies they are, they're just like naughty children," she laughs.

Mum and Dad help us to take the tent down. Flash, and Bella are standing quietly watching from a distance and are obviously waiting to be naughty again.

At last we have the tent folded up neatly which just leaves the ground sheet to deal with.

Before we realise, Bella has sneaked up behind us, grabbed hold of the corner of the sheet, and is cantering flat out around the field with her tail in the air.

Suddenly the long rubber material which is flapping loudly at the side of her has totally freaked her out and she is galloping faster and faster. She doesn't have the sense to open her mouth and let it go.

Flash is standing watching her behaviour in utter amazement.

Bella is now heading straight towards the post and rail fence at great speed. I'm rigid with fear as I can see what is going to happen. "Bella turn!" I bellow at the top of my voice, but she's going too fast and smashes into the fence with her chest hitting it with great force. She looks as if she has really winded herself and is brought to a sudden halt, her mouth drops open, and finally the sheet falls from her mouth. She looks completely stunned, she stands still for a few seconds, and is slowly walking across the field towards me. I walk towards her, I feel a little shaken up and worried she has hurt herself badly, but thankfully she seems to be walking ok.

I check her all over thoroughly, she seems none the worse for her accident, just a bit dazed. "Bella you are a silly pony," I gently chastise her as I plant a kiss on her muzzle and hug her tightly around her neck.

Dad slowly walks over to retrieve the ground sheet from where Bella had dropped it. He bends over to pick it up from the floor, turns around smiling but at this precise moment Bella gets spooked again and along with Flash off they go cantering then prancing around the field with their tails high in the air, snorting as they go. We make our way back to the bungalow for a drink and to calm down.

What an eventful day we have had.

Half an hour later we check our ponies and thankfully all is well.

# Chapter 26

* * *

AFTER SUCH AN EXHAUSTING DAY, we decide to get changed and ready for bed. We get some snacks from the kitchen to munch on whilst we have a good old chat.

We are happily eating a packet of crisps when from nowhere, Bella and Flash innocently appear at my bedroom window hoping for a titbit. Bella pushes back the curtain and sticks her head through.

"Oh no you don't," chuckles Sophie, as she gently pushes Bella back from the window, closes it and draws the curtains and at the same time shouts goodnight to both of them.

"I think we've had enough excitement for one day, don't you?" I say popping another crisp into my mouth.

"Great fun though," agrees Sophie, and turning out the light we both climb into bed.

* * *

The next day, Sophie and I re-site our tent in the back garden, and use parcel tape to repair the tear.

Satisfied that everything is ready and neat and tidy, we accompany Mum in the car so we can pick up my show jacket from the

Saddlery. It's lovely. A little long in the sleeves but this can be easily rectified. It fits perfectly everywhere else and is such a bargain. Although it is second hand it doesn't look like it's been used at all.

The next three days we have lots of fun practising for the show. We have received our schedule from Mrs Evans, and have chosen the classes we are going to enter. Completing the entry form we return it together with our entry money. I'm entering seven classes, and Sophie is entering six, so we are going to be very busy. It's a good thing we have strong healthy ponies.

I've chosen to enter the Mountain and Moorland class for unregistered ponies, 16 years and under, the 14.2h, the novice jumping class, and I may have a go at the clear round jumping but will decide for definite on the day. We have had such fun practising the gymkhana classes which we've been doing at 5.00pm when the sun isn't too hot.

Bella is funny at walk, trot, canter and lead. She will walk and trot nicely but when I ask her to canter, she gets too excited, we lose a couple of seconds whilst she's cantering on the spot when we should be going forward. Jumping off, I throw the reins over Bella's head and hope to make some time up on our way back with Bella pulling me along as I struggle to keep up with her. In practice Bella and I win eight times, and Sophie and Flash six.

We're also faster in the sack race as Sophie finds it impossible to jump in a sack without falling over, and of course we have fits of the giggles too which delays matters. Sophie hasn't entered this class anyway, saying she doesn't want to make a complete fool of herself, so it's not that important to her.

We have both entered the egg and spoon race, and we have been practising this on foot as well as on horseback. Sophie has beaten me every time but on our last practice I manage to come first. Sophie cannot believe my improvement; she is totally amazed and walks over to congratulate me only to find me laughing my head off as I stand holding the spoon upside down with the egg still on it! Yes, I admit I have cheated and super glued the egg onto the spoon! Sophie actually falls to the ground due to laughing so much!

The next class to practise is the flag race. We have to carry a flag whilst weaving in and out of poles, get to the far end, stand the flag in a bucket, canter back and repeat this three more times. Bella and I have become quite good at this one, we have been using road side cones to map out our course, and with all the practice we have done I'm feeling quietly confident about having a good chance in this one.

As Flash is a brilliant and confident jumper, Sophie has entered him in the 14.2h and over open class. She is also showing him in the Connemara class, and will take him in the clear round jumping class, plus three gymkhana classes.

It's a shame her parents won't be here to see her at the show, but both her Nan and Alan are coming, so she'll have support from them and of course me and my family.

# Chapter 27

* * *

TODAY IS FRIDAY AND ONLY two days to go until the show. We need to give our tack a really good clean. Sophie and I sit side by side in the tack room and decide it will be a lot easier if we shut the bottom door so we can crack on in peace. Flash and Bella, are standing looking over the door watching us intently. I'm sure they would love to come in and join us if they could.

Starting on our bridles, we hang them up and wipe them all over with a damp cloth, undoing all the buckles to ensure every bit of leather is clean. We remove the bits off the bridles and soak them in a bucket of warm, clear water. They aren't very dirty as we always rinse them after we return from every ride.

Next it's time for the saddle soap. Moistening the soap using a damp cloth we rub our bridles up and down, ensuring we do both sides properly.

Our next task is to clean our saddles. Sophie has a beautiful English leather saddle and as mine is synthetic, I have an easy task. We remove the girths which are made of cloth material, and soak them in warm soapy water; remove the stirrup leathers and irons, and Sophie starts on cleaning her saddle. We clean the stirrup irons separately with a metal polish.

We have done a fantastic job; in fact I would say perfect as we stand back to admire our hard work. We put the stirrup leathers and irons back on and all we have left to do is rinse our girths properly. This has all been a very tedious and time consuming job but is just one of those things that has to be done.

Bella, by this time is beginning to get very impatient probably due to the fact I haven't been paying her any attention. She bangs the tack room door a couple of times, and is certainly not impressed at being ignored.

"Give us two minutes and we will be with you", I call to her.

We stroll out into the yard to rinse off our girths and we hang them over the fence in the sun to dry and return to the tack room to clear everything up and put everything away. *Phew*, nearly done.

I stand and have a stretch, this has been quite a back aching job. Sophie is really thirsty and just as we turn to make our way back to the bungalow we suddenly stop in our tracks; we are horrified to see Bella pawing at the girths which are now sitting on the ground.

"No," I groan. "Now we'll have to wash them again!" Sophie giggles.

We re-soak and rinse the girths after brushing off the dry dust and hoof marks that Bella has so kindly put on them, and to be on the safe side we hang them on Mum's washing line, well away from our cheeky ponies.

# Chapter 28

* * *

By late afternoon our girths are dry and we decide it would be great to go to the riding school to practice our jumping.

I phone Mrs Evans to let her know we are coming over. I glance at my watch, 5.00pm. Mrs Evans is on hand to welcome us. Bella still gets very excited when jumping, and also enjoys giving the odd buck or two. She is very fast, and I know if we get through to a jump-off, we could stand a good chance, but I also realise I mustn't get too confident.

Flash is a great jumper, he is so much more controlled and sensible than Bella. He is more mature being a couple of years older than her. We have forty minutes practise in the school, thank Mrs Evans for all her help and leisurely ride home. "That was such great fun Sophie, you and Flash are amazing". Sophie responds, "Emily I really cannot believe what a truly amazing job you have done with Bella, from the very first day you saw her, you have always believed in her and she has always believed and trusted you." Sophie pauses to take a breath, "Just look at what you have achieved, you should both be very proud of yourselves. I truly am very proud of you both and I mean that from the bottom of my heart". I am now grinning like a Cheshire cat again and thank Sophie for the compliment. It really does mean a lot to me. We settle our ponies and head into the bungalow for a late dinner.

Today is Saturday, the day before the show. We are both feeling very excited and gabble away as we write a list of everything we need to remember to get ready for tomorrow.

Mum likes everything to be organised and is making sure we both have everything we need. She has taken charge of our clothes, and they're all hanging up ready and waiting.

Mum, Dad, and my grandparents are all coming to watch. Mum is putting a picnic together as it is going to be a long day for all of us.

The young handler showing classes will be first, starting at 9.30am, followed by the gymkhana at 12.30pm. The jumping is due to start at 2.30pm.

We decide to go for a short hack today as we don't want to tire them out before the show, and we are home by 5.00pm.

Time now to bath our ponies again. We have decided to leave them in the yard overnight as we do not want a repeat performance of what happened last time. We really hope they will try and stay reasonably clean to make our lives a little easier in the morning. Here we go again getting buckets and buckets of water. Nearly ready. Sophie calls our ponies, "Flash, Bella come on, time for another makeover at the salon".

Bella and Flash, are thankfully very good this time, it has only taken us around an hour to bath both of them and now we can tidy up. Sophie keeps complaining about how hot she is, so being the good friend I am, I decide to throw a bucket of cold water over her whilst she has her back turned. "Emily", she screeches. This really has taken her by surprise and has also taken her breath away. The water fight begins! I have two more buckets near me but I am not quick enough as Sophie has grabbed the hosepipe. I turn my back, "Sophie, no please don't I am sorry I didn't mean to throw the water over you, I just tripped and the bucket flew out of my hands". "Nice try Emily but that doesn't wash with me", she is in hysterics. I can feel the cold water firing at my back, on my legs, in my hair, and I need to escape quickly. I jump over the fence and run. "Spoil sport" I can hear Sophie calling. We are both totally drenched. "I will only come back if I see you have put the hosepipe away," I shout. I watch her at a distance whilst I get my breath back and I can see she has at last disconnected it and is now putting it safely back on the mount. I slowly walk towards her, she looks at the state of me and we collapse in fits of laughter. Bella and Flash are looking at us in utter disgust!

We clean our girths again, and wipe over our saddles and bridles, they look as good as new. We cheekily sneak our numnah's into Mum's washing machine as soon as she leaves to go out for a walk with Suki. Very naughty I know, but we decide it's a lot quicker than doing them by hand.

Forty minutes later I gallop back to the bungalow, take our numnah's out of the washing machine, and hang them to dry on the washing line. Hopefully Mum will be none the wiser! If she does find out, I know I'll be in big trouble!

Before going outside to sleep in our tent, we decide after the day we have had it would be heavenly to take a nice relaxing bath. "Sophie, I will go first as I know how long it takes you once you get in the bath with your lush bombs", "You are so cheeky Emily, what are you trying to say, are you saying I am dirtier than you?" I quickly reply, "Indeed I am, don't forget I had a good wash down with that cold hosepipe earlier, thanks to you!" "But Emily, you had your clothes on, how could that mean you have had a good wash?" blurts out Sophie in between laughing.

Eventually it is time for us to run through our checklist and we are thrilled to see everything is ready and in order. We are too excited to sleep so sneak back to the kitchen to raid the fridge and cupboards. We make our way quietly back to our tent carrying chocolate, apples, crisps and three bottles of water. We munch on our goodies and tell each other funny stories. "Hey Sophie this will really make you laugh. I am going to tell you about the time I offered to bath Rufus at the riding school, here goes, you will love this one."

"Rufus is a huge 16.2h horse but he's also known to be a bit of a wimp. I offered to give him a bath as Jodie was having a hectic day. I got everything ready and was feeling really positive. Off we went out to the field and I was thinking to myself, this won't take me long at all. I had the lunge line in my left hand and everything was going well until I put the wet sponge I was holding in my right hand onto his neck. He immediately panicked, the sponge dropped to the ground, I grabbed the lunge line with both hands, holding on with as much strength as I could muster. He bolted across the field leaving me running behind him trying to hang on for dear life. Rufus was obviously a lot stronger and faster than me, and to the on lookers it must have looked as if I was water skiing. I hung on to the end of the lunge line with every ounce of strength I had left with my legs flying in what seemed to be in all directions. It honestly felt like hours to me but was probably only about twenty seconds. I glanced out of the corner of my eye and saw three of the girls from the yard standing watching us, all laughing their heads off. I lost all concentration, my knees gave way, and I had no choice but to let go of the lunge line and I fell flat on my face! Rufus continued to run around the field with the lunge line still attached to his head collar, it was flying behind him like a snake on a mission. Thankfully before too long he tired and stopped and was none the worse for his escapade. I was really worried he would get tangled up in the lunge line and hurt himself." By this time Sophie is in hysterics, holding onto her ribs. 'Are you not going to ask how I was Sophie after my traumatic experience?' I muffle in between giggles. "Well for your information I was a bit bruised, had a few rope burns on my hands and also a black eye, but to be honest my pride was hurt more than anything". Sophie is now hunting for a tissue to wipe her tears away as they roll down her cheeks!

This story has been told many a time at the riding school, much to my continued embarrassment, but I can laugh about it now.

I set the alarm clock for 4.30am, and finally drift off to sleep to dream of our very first show.

# Chapter 29

* * *

Argh! There goes the alarm clock again, I'm already awake and switch it off as quickly as I can and at exactly the same time Sophie groans, "I'm still tired, it must still be the middle of the night, Emily please turn that noise off now."

I climb out of my sleeping bag and across to where Sophie is still snuggled down in hers, I shake her and cheerfully quip, "Come on Sophie, get up, today's the day. It's our first show."

"That's really exciting, but could I have another ten minutes please?" she mutters.

"You can stay where you are whilst I go and fetch us a nice hot cup of coffee, then you really must get up."

"Emily," murmurs Sophie. "I would love to know how you manage to be so wide awake, and cheerful every morning."

I bend over and pick up the empty chocolate wrappers and other odds and ends we had discarded the night before. I head for the kitchen, place these in the waste bin and put the kettle on to boil.

The mugs have been left out ready the night before, so all I have to do is place coffee into three mugs, and make a mug of tea for Dad. After taking theirs to them and giving Suki a kiss, I carry our coffee out to the tent and raise Sophie from her deep sleep. She's still mumbling and groaning about it being a ridiculous time to get up, and puts her head back inside her sleeping bag.

Sitting down on my sleeping bag and carefully placing the mugs safely to one side, I quietly say, "Sophie, if you don't surface in ten seconds I am going to fetch a bucket of very cold water and throw it all over you. That might help you to wake up!"

Maybe it is the tone of my voice or just the threat itself, but it certainly makes Sophie sit up and take notice. She knows only too well I am not joking, and before long we are both sitting up drinking our coffee.

"Good, now you're with it, how about some nice hot buttered toast?" I ask her.

"Sounds lovely."

"Come on then, bring your coffee," I say, as I stretch out a hand to pull her to her feet.

We finish breakfast, wash and dress, and we cannot believe it is now 5.30am. Time to rush out to see our ponies.

It's fairly light by now but we put the lights on anyway. Bella and Flash are resting together in the stable, they really do look cute, Flash has his head on Bella's back but they soon move quickly when they hear their breakfast coming.

Bella has a few manure stains around her quarters, and Flash a large stain on his neck.

"We'll have to wash these areas off, but it is not as bad as I expected," says Sophie.

Whilst the ponies are eating, we muck out the stable, fill their hay rack, and remove the droppings scattered around the yard.

Returning to the bungalow to fetch a bucket of warm water, Mum is in the kitchen singing away to her Michael Buble CD again and is in her element making piles of sandwiches.

"Hello love, do you need any help?" Mum asks.

"I think everything's under control at the moment Mum, but would you be able to keep an eye on Bella and Flash at around quarter to eight, so we can come in and get changed?"

"Of course I will love, just give me a shout when you want me."

I carry the water back out to the yard and we wash out all the stains from our ponies' coats.

"It was a good idea to keep them in last night after their baths. They smell so yummy from the herbal shampoo. I dread to think what they would have looked like this morning if we'd let them out in the field last night." I laugh.

The overnight stains washed off, we now start on the hard work of grooming. We want our ponies to shine, to gleam and to look as wonderful as possible.

A while ago Mrs James had given me a very helpful tip. She had told me to use a tea towel to rub all over Bella's coat. By rubbing hard all over the body in between strokes with the body brush, this brings the natural oil to the surface to give a smooth and shiny look. It certainly works well, and soon Bella's quarters look beautiful. I even manage 'shark teeth' quarter marks on her too but I will re-do these later just before we leave.

By now its 7.00am, and the sun is getting quite warm already. Dad appears and asks if we need any help.

"Oh yes please Dad," I reply gratefully. "Last night we didn't get around to picking up the droppings in the field, would you mind?"

"Right you are, happy to oblige," Dad says, and off he goes with the wheelbarrow and shovel.

I always remove the droppings from the field daily. Mrs Evans taught me this as she said it helps to stop worm infestation, and keeps the grazing clean. I bag up all of the manure and Nan and Grandad

H take it home to put on their roses. They say their roses bloom and are thriving from being fed Bella's manure, (they have actually named one of their roses Bella!) but to be honest just like the ants I'm not too sure whether or not to believe them.

I continue to groom Bella; her mane is tangle-free and is falling on the correct side at last. I've decided not to plait her mane today as she is entering a Mountain and Moorland class and apparently for this class ponies should be left with their mane flowing naturally. It's all very complicated! Mrs James has also explained that if I do plait Bella's mane I need to put an odd number up the neck and also one plait in the forelock. If you put an even number up the neck and one in the forelock you would actually lose marks in the class. *How bizarre*, I'd thought to myself at the time.

"Anything else you need doing?" asks Dad, reappearing after clearing the field.

"Thanks Dad," I reply gratefully. "Would you mind checking the water in the field? Also; the feed buckets need washing, and the feeds need making up ready for tonight."

"I know how to make Bella's feed up but I haven't a clue how to make up Flash's," he confesses in a slight panicky voice.

"Don't worry, Flash and Bella's menus are listed on the board in the tack room and all the feed bins are labelled, so I am sure you'll be fine," I assure him.

"If you say so," he replies chuckling as he heads off towards the tack room.

Sophie and I stand back, we are very pleased with how gorgeous our ponies look, and we are feeling very proud of them already. Both ponies have been thoroughly spoilt.

They've now received nearly two hours of pampering in our salon, their eyes and nostrils have been sponged, under their tails cleaned, and the final touch is to oil their hooves. Bella is very comical, "Bella, Mummy is going to paint your nails now," I say to her and immediately she puts one of her front hooves up on top of the upside-down bucket. She stands patiently whilst I varnish her nails! Sophie laughs, she finds this very amusing.

Dipping the bristles of the dandy brush in the bucket of water I gently brush Bella's mane and do the same to the top of her tail.

Now for the finishing touch. Sophie and I wipe herbal fly repellent around Flash and Bella's faces, on the top of their tails, and around the inside of their back legs.

"Not bad!" I hear a voice speak from nowhere. I turn around and see Mum smiling as she admires our two ponies.

"Oh no," I groan. "Is that the time already?"

"Yes love," replies Mum. "Suki's in the car waiting, so you must tell me what you want me to do. It's time for you two to go and get changed."

"Just stand and watch our ponies for us please Mum. Leave them tied up so they can't get up to any mischief whilst we're gone. We don't want them to ruin all our hard work."

"Off you trot then, we'll be fine." reassures Mum.

We make our way to the bungalow and I can hear Mum chatting away to our ponies. I turn and glance to see she is stroking Bella's neck. Bella is turning her head and looks as if she is giving Mum a kiss on her cheek. "Thank you Bella," she replies, giving her a kiss back.

Mum has always been wary of horses but since having Bella, her confidence has blossomed and she has told me she has truly fallen in love with her.

# Chapter 30

\* \* \*

Ten minutes later and we're ready.

"How smart do we look?" I say looking at Sophie. I'm wearing my black jodhpurs and white shirt, half-done-up tie, new Jodhpur boots, new velvet hat and my show jacket. I'm taking my cream jodhpurs to change into for the show jumping, Sophie also has her show outfit on, and she looks stunning.

We decide to wear jeans over our jodhpurs, to help keep them clean until our classes and as we make our way back outside Dad is busy loading up the car with the picnic, and he's telling Suki she mustn't touch anything.

"Come here, Emily." he says beckoning me over. "You look very lovely but I need to do your tie up properly. There, that's better. Now Sophie, let me check yours too," and he re-ties hers also. "You'd better let me know what else I have to take in the car," he continues. "I'll finish off here, and then I'll come over to the yard."

"I've put everything in my rucksack just over there Dad," I tell him pointing to the left.

My belly is starting to jump about with little butterflies. I hadn't thought that I might be nervous, and I am a little surprised.

"How are you feeling Sophie?" I ask, turning to face her.

"A little queasy," she admits pulling a face.

"Me too," I reply. "Come on, let's go and tell Mum know we're ready."

"Hey Mum, I hope they've been good."

"Proper little angels," she replies. "It's as if they know today is a special day and I'm sure they're going to be on their best behaviour."

I reach for the body brush and replace the 'shark teeth markings' onto Bella's quarters. We both tack up our ponies, and we're almost ready to go. Those butterflies are starting to flutter again.

Bella's head collar has already been packed into my rucksack together with my first aid kit, a lead rope, and a few grooming items including a hoof pick.

We're just about to leave when Mum comes running out of the bungalow.

"Emily, I've just checked your list, have you got the veterinary certificates with you?" she asks.

"Oh, Mum, it's a good job you remembered. I've left them on my bedside cabinet, what am I like?" I call back.

"Don't worry I'll go and fetch them, and put them safely in my handbag."

It's now 8.30am, we're about to leave when Mum appears with her camera and starts clicking away. Dad is making sure everything is locked up safely, and at last we are on our way.

* * *

We arrive at the entrance to the show, it is at the opposite end to the riding school yard. The fields are a hive of activity already, ponies whinnying, horse boxes, trailers and people everywhere.

Bella's ears are alert with excitement. She starts to prance. I pat her neck and speak gently to her, Bella immediately responds by calming down.

I've read many books on animal psychology, and I was very interested to learn how sensitive animals can be. In fact, so much so, they can easily pick up on how we are feeling. If the rider is relaxed, then the horse or pony will be too. If the rider feels nervous or anxious they will sense this, and feel the same. I really have to remember to take a lot of deep breaths today.

I can see two large show rings marked out. In another direction what looks to be the gymkhana area, and over in the far distance three superb rings full of colourful and awesome show jumps.

Suddenly we hear a deep voice over the loud speaker, "If you haven't already registered, please make your way over to the secretary's tent."

Sophie and I ride across the field, and stop to ask where the secretary's tent is as we need to pick up our numbers and show our veterinary certificates.

Mum and Dad are already waiting there for us, and spotting us, Mum waves our veterinary certificates in the air.

We dismount and hand both ponies over to Mum and Dad, and make our way to the tent.

It doesn't take us long as we have already sent in our forms and paid for our entries and soon we are back, proudly carrying our numbers. Mine is 147 and Sophie's is number 197.

I hand the veterinary certificates straight back to Mum and she puts them into her handbag for safe keeping. She helps us pin our numbers onto our jackets, we remount and at last we are ready.

# Chapter 31

*  *  *

My first class is in ring one at 9.30am, so we decide to have a quick ride around.

"Meet us at ring one at 9.20am," I call out to Mum and Dad, and they both raise an arm in acknowledgement.

The smell of burgers fill the air. A little girl around the age of four is eagerly tucking into a burger, and her face is already covered in tomato sauce. The little girl's mum is running across towards her, "Oh no, Lucy. I told you that you have to try and keep clean, how many more times do I have to tell you," she screeches as she tries in vain to wipe the sauce from her daughter's face with a screwed-up tissue.

Sophie and I look at each other and can't help but giggle.

A familiar voice reaches our ears.

"How marvellous the pair of you look, dears," a beaming Mrs Evans says. "How are you feeling? A little nervous, I would say."

We both nod.

"Don't worry, that is quite normal, dears," continues Mrs Evans. "You're here to enjoy yourselves, and to have fun. Try to relax, and remember to take lots of deep breaths."

I am very relieved to see Mrs Evans has put her lipstick on perfectly this morning!

"Well dears, I must fly. Good luck, see you later," and off she rushes.

I glance at my watch and see it's now 9.18am, "Come on, Sophie, we'd better get to ring one."

Mum and Dad are already waiting for us.

"I need to go to the toilet," I confess.

"Me too," adds Sophie.

We both rush off, leaving Mum and Dad holding our ponies once again.

The first class is an in-hand class, I have to take Bella's saddle off. I remove my jeans to reveal my clean black jodhpurs. Mum tucks my hair into my hair net, which thankfully is another item she'd put into her handbag at the last minute, and I put my hat back on. Bella is looking brilliant.

"All entries for young handler, 16 years and under, to ring one now please," announces the same deep voice over the loudspeaker.

My tummy jumps nervously, and for a moment I think I need the toilet again. Taking a big deep breath, Mum, Dad, and Sophie wish me luck as I head off into the ring to see there are 17 entries in this class.

Bella's head is held very high as I lead her around the outside of the ring. One by one, each entrant is asked to come to the centre of the ring, walk away from the judge, and trot back.

Soon it's our turn. I remember it's important to stay by Bella's shoulder even though I'm tempted to run by her head. Bella trots beautifully, and to be honest I think we've done very well. I am asked to walk Bella around the show ring, I am told to stop and stand. I wait nervously and take some deep breaths. "Thank you," says the judge, before calling the next entrant. I gently stroke Bella, and tell

her how proud I am of her as we stand patiently watching the other entrants have their turn. The judge looks at the last pony and two minutes later a different voice is making an announcement over the loud speaker. She is the assistant to the judge and is calling out certain numbers. "Will numbers 252, 198, 275, 42 and 147 come forward please."

I am totally stunned as it suddenly dawns on me I am number 147, I am grinning like a Cheshire cat as I proudly lead Bella across to stand opposite the judge, alongside four other ponies.

The judge awards a 'special' rosette to the 5th place, a beautiful Welsh looking pony and now she's walking straight towards us. My heart is pounding. Patting Bella on her neck, she turns to me,

"Well done, what a gorgeous pony you have," and she hands me a beautiful silky green rosette with 4th printed in the centre. I can feel myself beaming. I can't believe it, our first rosette. My birthday wish has come true.

In the distance, I can hear Mum shouting, "Well done Emily, and Bella!" together with lots of clapping, and a couple of barks, which I guess is Suki. I pat Bella and whisper, "Bella what a clever girl you are. I really am so proud of you and I love you so much". I hug her tight and plant a kiss on her soft muzzle. The ponies and their handlers are now asked to leave the ring, and I proudly turn and lead Bella patting her repeatedly on her neck whispering, "Well done my girl, I love you."

Mum and Dad rush over to hug me, and also a big hug for Bella.

Sophie rides across. "Congratulations you two," she says, grinning down at us. "I have to go to ring two now for my first class. Fingers crossed I'll do as well as you."

"I'll be over to watch you in a second," I promise. "Good luck."

Sophie does very well in the Connemara class. She has a blue rosette for coming second. She says she can't believe it, she had felt so nervous and was sure the judge could hear her heart pounding.

Sophie's Nan has filmed the class on a camcorder, so Sophie's Mum and Dad will be able to watch it when they arrive back from holiday. Alan has also turned up, and gives Sophie a big well done kiss. She's beaming.

# Chapter 32

\* \* \*

My NEXT CLASS IS AT 10.30am in ring two. The Mountain and Moorland class is for unregistered native breeds. Once again I have to take off Bella's saddle, and repeat the same procedure as I did in the first class. This time the judges take a very long time, maybe due to there being 32 entries in this class. Bella is getting very bored and agitated, she is putting her head in the air and not behaving as well as she did in our first class.

Eventually the first five are selected by the judge and all five look to be pure Welsh-bred ponies. I have to admit they all look fantastic and moved and behaved perfectly. No rosette for me but maybe next time.

The gymkhana classes are due to start at 12.30pm so Mum and Dad decide it is probably best to have an early lunch.

We return to where Dad has parked our car and Mum carefully lays out the picnic. Sophie has taken Flash for a drink but is soon back with us. Bella has already had a drink on the way to the car from one of the big black bins which are positioned more or less everywhere full of fresh water. She is so funny, she kind of blows her nose in it, and finds it very amusing when bubbles appear, then she snorts at them!

Sophie and I remove our saddles, put on their head collars and lead ropes. Keeping hold of the lead ropes, we let them graze contentedly whilst we all enjoy our sandwiches.

I can sense Bella is sneaking up behind my shoulder, I can sense her breath and can feel her head leaning over me, she is stretching her neck trying to reach my cucumber and salad cream sandwich. She has a smidge of salad cream on her tongue and curls up her lip, shakes her head and doesn't try to pinch it again! She certainly isn't keen on my choice of sandwiches.

'Bella you are so funny', I say to her.

Both sets of my grandparents arrive, and I tell them how well we've done so far. Nan, and Grandad D take a photo of me and Bella with our rosette.

It's now 12.00pm and time to warm up Bella, we are ready to have some fun in the gymkhana classes. Our first class is the sack race. We win our first heat, and hooray we're through to the final.

We all watch the following heat, one poor girl falls over in her sack, and her pony accidentally treads on her arm. The first aid people are called immediately but sadly she is taken off to casualty with a suspected break. Oh dear.

Now it's time for the six finalists. Bella is very excited, and is cantering on the spot again. The whistle blows and Bella jumps forward, putting in a very large buck. I can vaguely hear spectators laughing. Squeezing Bella on with my legs, we manage to make up some ground, and arrive at the other end in one piece. I jump off Bella as quickly as I can, I'm in the sack and jump for all I'm worth. We're now in third place and need to make up some ground. The girl in front, unfortunately for her, falls over, I naughtily smile. I am now in second place with only one to catch. I'm breathing very heavily, and I am seriously getting out of breath. In the background I vaguely hear voices shouting and cheering us on. Bella is sensing my excitement, she suddenly jerks me and my sack to the left, I'm losing my balance, too late, I fall flat on my face. I don't know how but I'm still hanging onto the reins. Thankfully Bella stops as soon as I hit the deck. I just have to lay still for few seconds, I do feel a bit winded. I carefully move my limbs making sure all my body parts can move. Slowly, I get to my feet and step out of the sack, pat Bella on her neck to let her know all is ok, and walk out of the ring. I haven't won, but at least we're both in one piece.

Only my pride is dented. I can hear people cheering for the winner and Bella is looking at me with a very sad expression on her face. I give her a big hug to reassure her. "Never mind Bella, please don't look so worried," I say soothingly. "It was fun taking part wasn't it?"

Mum and dad come rushing over. "Are you alright Emily love, does anything hurt?"

"No, I'm fine thank you, and so is Bella. To be honest I just feel a bit stupid really."

Sophie arrives and just typical of her, takes one look at me and bursts into giggles, she sets me off too.

"I'm sorry Emily, I know I shouldn't laugh, but you were truly spectacular the way you went down, spread eagled, flat on your face, wow, absolutely awesome, that is the reason I didn't enter as I didn't want to make a fool of myself!" she blurts out in between trying to stifle her giggles. "Thank you for being so supportive Sophie", I say sarcastically.

The next gymkhana class is the walk, trot, canter and lead race. Once again Bella, and I reach the final.

The whistle blows for the final, and we're off! Bella walks beautifully, we're all level pegging as we turn around the far cone to start trotting back; Bella goes straight into a canter and I have to turn her in a circle, we've lost a bit of time. Now it's time to canter back. We're in fourth position, I urge Bella forward and she does an almighty buck. We are meant to be cantering but she is gathering speed, and if

I don't try and steady her quickly we will be going into a full-blown gallop. She's full of excitement, I gently tug at the reins and I am now back in control as I realise we are now in third position at the next cone. I jump off Bella, throw the reins over her head and set off as fast as I can. Bella is cantering at my side and I'm running as fast as my legs will carry me. The finishing line quickly appears. Yes, we've done it! We've come second. "Hooray!" I hear Mum shout,

"Woof, woof," I hear Suki bark again. I need to get my breath back before we are presented with our rosette.

"Thank you," I manage to say to the sponsor as a royal blue rosette with '2nd' printed on the centre is presented to me. Words cannot tell you how proud I am of Bella.

The next two classes we have entered are the egg and spoon race and the flag race.

In the egg and spoon race, can you believe after all of the practice I had with Sophie last week, I drop my egg in the first heat! It's a pity I couldn't have super glued it to the spoon as this would have given me a great chance!

In the flag race we sail through to the final but I fumble and drop my flag and have to dismount to pick it up. Bella decides to dance around; this is making it very difficult for me to get back on and when I eventually do, we finish last.

Sophie and Flash have done really well. They've come third in the bending race and second in the egg and spoon. To be honest I'm not sure how she has managed this so I ask her for proof, "Show me your egg and spoon, I need to check they're not stuck together." Her cheeky response is to stick her tongue out at me! Sophie hasn't done any good in the flag race either but she said it was good fun.

# Chapter 33

* * *

IT'S NOW 1.30PM, AND TIME for a well-earned rest.

Luckily, even though it's a very warm day, the clouds are mostly covering the sun, so it's ideal conditions for us all. I walk across to the outside tap and fill up a bucket of fresh water and offer it to Bella and Flash, but they don't seem bothered.

Bella feels very warm after her exertions in the gymkhana games, and as she won't drink out of my water bucket I lead her over to the big black bins of water. She blows again at the water, bubbles appear and she snorts again! I truly love my Bella, she always makes me smile. I hand Bella to Dad so I can rush off to change into my cream jodhpurs.

My next class is not until 2.30pm. This is the 14.2 h and under novice jumping, the class I have been really looking forward to. I return in my nice cream jodhpurs and sit down on a towel to keep them clean. I can now relax a little until 2.00pm and we can then go across to watch the clear round jumping. Mum and Dad have disappeared to watch the lead rein classes; they think the little children dressed up in their riding clothes look very cute. Bella's head is gently resting over my shoulder, and I smile.

As I sit, I see a little girl heading towards us riding a lovely Exmoor pony. She has an ice cream cornet in one hand, and I know I've seen her before. It isn't until she's closer to me, and I can see her face clearly, that a big grin spreads across my face. Thought so, she still has dried red tomato sauce all around her chin, and now ice cream dripping down her clothes. She really is in a world of her own. I wonder what her Mum will say when she catches up with her daughter?

Stopping directly in front of me and Bella, she points to her pony's head.

"Look," she says proudly. "Brandy and me, won three rosettes."

"That's wonderful," I reply, smiling at her. "Well done to both of you. Which classes did you win?"

The little girl obviously isn't sure. She just shrugs her shoulders, turns away and continues to ride her pony towards the opposite ring.

Now it's time for me and Bella to go across to the clear round jumping. Sophie and Flash are standing looking focussed and confident waiting for their turn to enter the ring.

"What do you think Bella? Do you fancy having a go at this one?" I ask her looking straight into her eyes. I'm sure she winks at me. "Come on then," I say and we rush across to the secretary's tent once more.

"Hello Emily," greets Mrs Montgomery, one of the helpers for the day. "Fancy entering this one, do you?"

"Yes please. Is it too late to add my name?"

"Not at all. Emily Pope isn't it, and your number is?"

"Number 147," I reply.

"There you are Emily," she says as she writes my name and number on the list. "Just wait for your name to be called and good luck."

"Thank you," I grin, and hurry back to watch Sophie and Flash.

How professional the two of them look. Flash just glides over the jumps and makes it look so easy. Sophie proudly rides out of the ring with a clear round rosette.

"Well done Sophie, and of course you Flash," I say as I stroke his neck. "You did that beautifully. I've just put my name down to have a go, so I'll see you later. I just want to warm Bella up a bit."

I ride Bella over to a quiet piece of land, and start our warm up. I pop her over a little cavaletti jump first, and then a much larger one. Bella clears them easily. Suddenly, I hear the same deep voice over the loud speaker.

"Emily Pope and Bella, please make your way to the clear round jumping ring."

Earlier in the day, Sophie and I had quickly walked the course to make sure Sophie knew the order of the jumps. I'm so glad I had walked it with her.

Bella and I enter the ring at a trot, the bell rings and we are off. Ten jumps in total and all have to be jumped clear. The first three are easy but at the fourth jump Bella gets too close to the top pole and it crashes to the ground. I quickly collect Bella up, we clear the tyre jump, only five to go, four to go, three to go, two to go, and on the last jump Bella refuses. "Oh dear, never mind Bella," I say to her soothingly. "We just need a little more practice. Great fun though wasn't it?"

Sophie is waiting to greet us as we come out of the ring, "Don't worry Emily, when Bella is in the mood, she can really jump. Just try to relax and try to enjoy yourself."

"Ok matey," I reply, grinning back at her. "After all it's our first show, and I'm already very proud of her."

It's now 2.20pm, and only ten minutes to go until our last class.

There are 26 entries in all so Bella and I have a lot of competition. I'm eighth to jump and a clear round will get us through to the jump-off. The 14.2 h and over jumping class has also started in another ring. Flash, and Sophie, are listed as tenth to go in their round, and once again the number of entries is high, 22 in this class.

# Chapter 34

$*\ *\ *$

"Here we go Bella, this is the big one. Do your best," I say to her softly.

We enter the ring and slowly canter around until we reach the starting line and we're off. The first jump is a three-foot parallel followed by a double, a false wall, around the corner over a double, only five more jumps to go.

"Good girl Bella!" I manage to say, although I'm a bit puffed as we turn into the bend into the final straight in a lovely canter, Bella puts in a huge buck and for a few seconds I lose concentration but

manage to quickly get back on track. We clear the final three jumps with ease. A clear round, this is brilliant, in fact beyond my wildest dream!

"We're through Bella, we're through!" I shout joyfully leaning forward to pat her on her neck.

I realise my arms are really aching, Bella is so keen to jump, sometimes I really do struggle to hold her back.

Mum, Dad, and my grandparents are waiting to congratulate us as we exit the ring. I thank them all, dismount Bella and lead her across to the other ring just in time to watch Sophie and Flash achieve a clear round too. We cheer like mad, and return back to the 14.2h and under ring to watch our competition. Loosening Bella's girth for a while, we try to relax.

Mrs Evans arrives to give me some advice for the jump-off.

"Take it steady for the first half of the course dear, speed up over the double, check Bella on the final bend, and then let her go at her own pace coming to the final three jumps. The last run is where you'll pick up any lost time. Good luck dear," she says, and disappears quickly.

I know I'll have trouble holding Bella back, but I also know she has a lot of speed. By the time the 26 entrants have finished, its 3.45pm and I'm eager to see how many have got through to the final. Only six! We've been drawn fourth to jump.

The jump-off is just about to start in Sophie's class. There are eight in total with Sophie jumping last. Sophie and I wish each other good luck, and I ride back to our ring to watch the first entry. A young man and his pony Conker finish in a very fast time of one minute and six seconds but they have four faults having knocked down the first part of the double. The next entrant manages a clear round, but is slower with a time of one minute and twenty seconds.

The third pair in the ring have a refusal which gives them three faults, and a slower time of one minute and twenty four seconds.

Now it's our turn. I check my girth and concentrate on my breathing. Entering the ring I'm hoping we look confident, although the butterflies in my stomach are having their own jump off.

The bell rings and we're off. We complete the first half of the course with no problems, although Bella is once again pulling very hard. The next jump clear, and Bella is now going at a very fast pace. I desperately try to collect her up as best as I can before we go around the corner to enter the last three jumps in the straight.

I pull hard on the reins, I just know we're going too fast and as we hit the bend, Bella loses a hind leg and goes down onto her knees, but somehow she manages to scramble back up with me hanging onto anything I can grab. It's all happening so quickly, but I'm now back in my seat, and Bella is flying at the final three jumps for all she's worth. All I can do is sit and let Bella take charge. Jump eight clear, jump nine clear, one more to go, Bella is going so fast, she literally runs straight through the last jump. I struggle to pull her up, we have 4 faults but Bella has done so well, I'm so proud.

Even though my ears seem to be ringing, I manage to hear the time announced, "One minute, eight seconds." We would have taken the lead if we hadn't gone through the last jump costing us 4 faults, but at least we're in second place, and more importantly in one piece.

I ride Bella out of the ring, and realise my hands are really shaking. *'Must be the adrenalin'* I think to myself. Mrs Evans is running towards me in a very excited manner.

"What a top performance Emily, dear. Well done to you both. You did very well to sit the final bend, and what a star Bella is to pick herself up like that and take charge. Shame about the last jump but Bella will calm down as she gets older, and this experience will have done her the world of good."

I slowly dismount and realize my legs are shaking uncontrollably, they give way as my feet touch the ground and I sit down with a thump. Is this more adrenalin running through my body I wonder as I sit there? Bringing my knees up to my chin, I hug my legs in the hope the shaking will soon stop.

I stay where I am and look up to see Bella's face looking at me in a very concerned manner. She's standing in front of me with her head bowed, and I swear she is thinking, *'whatever are you doing down there again!'* I'm just too tired to laugh, and lower my head again. Bella nuzzles my cheek, and I feel her breathing heavily through her nostrils.

Mum and dad with Suki close to Mum's side, come running over. Mum blurts out, "Oh, Emily, love, you gave us such a fright out there for a minute, but very well done. Here, let me hold Bella while you have a drink of water. You look quite pale."

At this exact moment, I hear the spectators groan. The fifth rider has knocked down two fences, and has eight faults. We are still in second place.

Only one pony and rider left to jump. I just have to get up to watch this.

"Dad, will you help me up please?" I ask, reaching out to clasp his hand. He pulls me to my feet, and I have to hang on to his arm to steady myself. Turning towards the ring, I watch the last entry walk confidently into the ring.

# Chapter 35

* * *

STAR GAZING IS A BEAUTIFUL Palomino, and his rider is totally focussed as they enter the ring.

I can hardly bare to watch as they easily clear everything in their stride, only the last three to jump and my heart is truly pounding. Jump eight clear, nine clear, now for the final jump and I hold my breath. Star Gazing clears the last jump with ease and has managed a truly awesome time of 1 minute and 3 seconds. These two are most definitely the winners.

A voice over the loudspeaker is making an announcement. "The winner of the 14.2 and under novice jumping is Star Gazing, in 2nd place Conker, in 3rd place Bella and in 4th place Shadow."

"Go on Emily, off you two go," urges Dad.

I can't believe it; we've got third place. What a long way Bella has come.

With help from Dad, I manage to mount and ride into the ring with the three other riders and their ponies. My legs still feel wobbly but at least I'm sitting on Bella, and don't have to walk into the ring. I'm in a daze, and still can't believe it.

We're beckoned into the centre of the ring. The sponsor of the class walks across to the rider and pony who have finished in fourth place, and presents them with their rosette together and a small size silver cup.

It's my turn now and the lady sponsor is walking towards us. She holds out her hand to me and I eagerly shake it, then she pats Bella's neck, "Really well done to the pair of you. What an exciting jump-off you gave us. It was a shame about the last jump, but such a superb effort," she says.

She is pinning a treble-layer rosette onto Bella's bridle, and is now handing me a medium silver cup, I am instantly beaming again like a Cheshire cat. I'm just so proud of my Bella, and outside the ring I can hear my family clapping and cheering loudly, together with a little bark or two.

I am truly buzzing; this feeling is truly amazing. If only I could bottle this feeling up and sell it, I'd be very, very rich.

Eventually Bella and I ride out of the ring, and are greeted by my family and what a wonderful surprise to see Mrs James and Toddy too. Mum and Dad hug me as much as they can, so much so that they nearly pull me off Bella! Mum is sniffling; she's obviously shed some tears! Soppy so and so.

Bella lays her head over Mum's shoulder, and what a very special moment this is. Smiling at everyone, I try to stop a tear but it is too late, it has escaped and is rolling down my cheek. *'I am such a soppy so and so too'* I think to myself!

# Chapter 36

**\* \* \***

Suddenly, we hear another loud cheer, and look across to the other ring just in time to see Sophie and Flash clear the last jump.

We can't believe it. Sophie and Flash have finished in second place, only beaten by 0.5 of a second. How close is that?

I urge Bella forward, and with everyone following behind us we manage to reach the ring just in time to cheer on Sophie, as she proudly accepts her trophy and rosette.

We clap and cheer as loudly as we can as Sophie and Flash ride out of the ring.

"So close Sophie, bad luck. That is the closest jump off I've ever seen. Well done! You should be very proud of yourself, dear," says Mrs Evans, and Sophie beams with pride.

What a fantastic day we've had. It's beyond my wildest dreams and I feel like I'm on cloud nine as I hold my trophy tight, the one I've dreamed of winning for so many years. Although we didn't win this time, it's still only our first show and Bella looks very proud wearing her 2$^{nd}$, 3$^{rd}$ and 4$^{th}$ rosettes.

Sophie and I pose on our ponies so Mum, and everyone else with a camera can happily snap away at the four of us with our trophies and rosettes.

Sophie's Nan has managed to get most of our classes on her camcorder, including our jump-off and has arranged with Mum to bring the DVD over to us tomorrow evening so we can all re-live this very special day. I am really looking forward to watching Sophie's jump off.

Mrs Evans is now rushing towards me and she wraps her arms around me tightly giving me a massive hug which almost takes my breath away.

Soon it's time for me and Sophie to set off on our short journey home. We say our goodbyes and I jump off quickly to give Toddy a big cuddle. "Mrs James it's so lovely to you again, thank you so much for coming today to cheer us on, you must come over and see us very soon". I am taken by surprise as Mrs James totally out of the blue also gives me a massive hug and is whispering in my ear how proud she is of us all. Another tear threatens.

I jump back on Bella, and even though Sophie and I are feeling completely worn out, we manage to chat all the way home, we are on such a high! We laugh about the sack race, and I'm sure Sophie won't let me forget that for a very long time. Friends eh!

# Chapter 37

* * *

It's nearly 6.00pm by the time we arrive home, and we are so relieved to see Mum and Dad are waiting in the yard to give us a hand. We un-tack our ponies whilst Mum and Dad carry our tack to the tack room. We pick out their feet and let them tuck into their well-earned dinner. Once they have finished eating we turn them out into their paddock and in unison they both get down for a well-deserved roll, first to the left, then to the right, up they get having a jolly good shake.

They look so content after such a long day, and must be just as tired as we are, if not more so. We make up their feeds ready for the morning, lock up the yard, and walk slowly back to the bungalow, (no galloping back there today!). Time now, for a nice hot bath, me first, whilst Mum is cooking the dinner. We're both really shattered, we put our PJ's on before dinner. I'm sure Mum and Dad won't mind just this once!

I proudly stick my rosettes on my bedroom wall with blue tack, just as I've always dreamed of doing and put my shiny silver trophy on top of my cabinet. I just about have enough energy for my cheesy grin to appear. We all sit down to eat dinner, and chat constantly about today's events. Bella, and I have won 3 rosettes and a trophy.

Sophie and Flash have won five rosettes and of course their trophy. What a lot Sophie will have to tell her parents when they get back from their holiday, although I suspect she's already text them as she was very busy on her phone earlier.

It's now 8.00pm and to be honest we are ready for bed. Sophie and I walk out to the paddock still in our PJ's and slippers to say goodnight to Bella and Flash. Their water container is nearly empty so Sophie and I each fill up a bucket to top it up. We give them both a carrot, and hug them goodnight.

Time now for us to head off to bed. I snuggle down in my sleeping bag, and within two minutes of turning off the portable light I'm fast asleep. I dream of our very first show, my beautiful pony Bella, and also of future adventures to come, especially our visit to Aunty Pam's.

## The End

Printed in Great Britain
by Amazon